UNFORGIVABLE

CAROL RAYYAN

ACKNOWLEDGMENTS

A big thanks again to my wonderful friend and editor Noah Ross for teaching me how to flesh out the mystical world that is The Hidden City. You are a gifted writer.

Thanks to my test audience: Michelle, Laura, Kristina, Joanna and Nicole. Your support has been amazing.

And finally, to my incredible husband Isa. I dedicate this book to you. I could not have done this without your constant encouragement and strength. You are my real dream come true.

PROLOGUE

I was running down a dark path, branches cracking beneath my bare feet. Vertical hedges rose toward the sky around me, as I struggled to find my way out.

The prophecy states that on her 25th birthday she will awaken. I heard this echoing in my mind.

I ran my hands frantically along the hedge walls hoping to find a breach in the pattern; some kind of short cut out, but each turn I took led me to a dead end.

She will have hair black as night and eyes blue as the ocean.

My breathing labored, my heart raced with fear as I heard my pursuers closing the distance. I tried to run quietly, but the branches snapped below my every step and jagged twigs dug into the soles of my feet, leaving a trail of blood behind me. I had nowhere to hide.

She will have powers no single witch has ever had.

I doubled back the way I had come and ran quickly around the other side of the hedge before I could be spotted.

She will stop the dark ones from conquering all the good witches in our world.

I found a stretch of the maze laid before me illuminated only by the waning moon and I ran down it head long.

No, that can't be me. I thought. Then I remembered my mother's note, her letter from beyond the grave.

We bound your powers for your protection... the spell will wear off on your 25th birthday.

The others were coming, I could feel their eyes on my back, hear their breathing and heavy footfalls.

I stopped and spun around to confront them, only to find Tristan and Lexi standing there.

Alexis was chosen to watch over you when you were just a child. My mother's words rang in the night air. *You may have already met Tristan; he was also assigned to protect you.*

Behind them I saw the rushing figures of Crystal and Yuri.

I tried to warn my friends, but no words came out. I swung my arms to conjure a fierce wind to throw my enemies back, but my whirlwind spell didn't work. I felt suddenly weak and fell to my knees just as Crystal and Yuri pounced on Tristan and Lexi.

No, that's not right. That's not the way it happened. I knew then that I was dreaming, and the images changed course to match that of my memories. Crystal and Yuri standing at the camp site. The other rogue witches fighting Tristan, Lexi, Genevieve, Lachlan and I, spells flying, lighting the dark night, and blood spilling, pooling on the ground. I heard Yuri's wailing as Tristan cut off his finger, saw Crystal's eyes blazing as she watched. Their incineration, when I had used all the hurt and anger and fear inside of me to defeat them once and for all, blazed strong in my mind. I remembered my mother's enchanted ring that she gave me for comfort, showing me that killing them was necessary and had saved lives, and remembered my guilt ebbing.

My memories spiraled with anger as I thought of the person responsible for all my torment. Darien. I saw the rabid bats he sent me splattering across my front door, how he destroyed my apartment by making the earth tremble, made me imagine I was being consumed by bugs as their tiny, dirty feet touched my skin, and finally sending Crystal and Yuri after us. The fear that we didn't know where Darien was or what he was going to do to us.

I bolted up in bed. I turned my bedside lamp on to wash away the darkness and drank the water that I had left on the stand. I leaned my head against the headboard and waited for my breathing to calm. The lamp shook from my fear and I steadied it.

My whole world would have been rocked regardless when I found out I was a witch, but to find out I was a witch with superior powers, that I was destined to defeat a dark witch and his followers was a good deal more than anyone could have prepared me for.

I couldn't say that I hadn't enjoyed all these powers, and though I was still in the process of developing them, I was having fun with the ones I already had. I just wished people weren't out to kill me because of them.

If it hadn't been for that warning, we may have all died. I still didn't know who had sent me the visions showing me that Darien was sending an army after us, but I was grateful to him every day.

We hadn't heard from Darien, and we didn't know where he was or what he was up to, though we were always alert.

I knew it wasn't over. Not by a long shot. No, this was just getting started.

1. SALE-ABRATION

"Selena," Lexi sing-songed.

I opened my eyes to see her standing beside the bed, bouncing from one foot to the next. Her short, blond hair was styled in spikes with the lone pink streak the center of attention and her brown eyes sparkled with excitement.

"Don't you ever knock anymore?" I asked, sitting up.

"Oh come on, you know I can get in anytime I want." She wiggled her fingers. Lexi could open and protect places so her fingers were like a master key.

I rolled my eyes. "I know, but it's common courtesy." I looked at Lexi beaming and knew she didn't care. "Fine, what is it." I got out of bed and headed for the bathroom while Lexi talked. Thankfully my apartment had been restored after the earthquake destroyed it. The insurance covered the repairs and I sped the process along with my magic.

"You get a day off today," she cheered.

"Really?" I asked. I hadn't had a day off from training in a while since we never knew when Darien would strike. I squirted paste on the toothbrush and started scrubbing my teeth clean.

"Yes, really," Lexi said. "So, we're going shopping to buy outfits for my birthday."

"Lexi, you're birthday is in three days," I said over a mouthful of foam. "And you don't even know how you're going to celebrate it. What would we even buy?" I spat out the excess.

"Something sexy. I'm sure we'll go somewhere fun." Her eyes gleamed.

"Fine… I'd rather shop than train." I rinsed my mouth and threw some water on my face.

"Great! Oh, and Tristan is going to come with us for extra protection."

My stomach fluttered. "Great," I said much less enthuseiastically than Lexi had, as I dried my face.

"Hurry up," she said. "We will need all the time we can get."

"Lexi, it's still early, can't I have some coffee first?" I walked to the kitchen already deciding that I *would* have coffee whether Lexi liked it or not.

"Fine," she huffed as she sat down at the kitchen table. She was so anxious to leave and looked so sad, I almost laughed.

"I tell you what," I said as I turned the coffee machine on. "I will get dressed while the coffee brews; that way I can save some time. Deal?"

Lexi smiled, "Deal."

I went to my room, threw on a pair of jean shorts and a breezy white shirt. It was summertime in Arizona, and the heat was flirting ridiculously around the 120 degree mark. I brushed my black hair and let it fall to my waist, dabbed just a touch of mascara on my eyelashes, and slapped on some deodorant and a spritz of perfume. I looked at my reflection and into my sapphire blue eyes. I looked good enough; it was just the mall.

Walking back to the kitchen I heard a knock on my door.

"I'll get it," Lexi called. I didn't have to wonder who it was, there was only one other person who would come here this early. Tristan. I ignored the anticipation that his presence elicited and was glad I changed out of my pajamas.

I walked into the living room just in time to see Lexi closing the door behind Tristan. He strode in as if he owned the place and sat on the couch. His brown hair was stylishly messy, and his yellow-specked green eyes glimmered in the morning light from the window. He gave me a lazy smile as I entered the room and my heart fluttered. Damn him and his stupid rules.

I remembered how Tristan had invaded my life. He showed up out of the blue and told me he was sent to protect me. When I tried to date Darien (I know, but I didn't know he was super evil at the time,) Tristan warned me against it, but I didn't listen. Now I was in love with Tristan, and although he had expressed some emotion toward me, that hadn't prevented him from laying down ground rules: no romance. We had to have boundaries, so he could have a clear head and protect me. It was bull, but whatever. Since then we had been professional, and he had been training me to use my physical strength, while Lexi had been training me to control my powers. I pushed the memory aside.

"Hey," I said casually. I walked past him and into the kitchen. I poured myself a cup of coffee and sat beside Lexi at the table.

"So, you excited to go shopping?" I asked Tristan with fake enthusiasm.

He raised his eyebrow. "Yeah," he said sarcastically.

"Come on guys," Lexi chirped. "This will be fun! We need to get out more."

"What we need is to go after him," Tristan said, sitting up straight.

"Well, yeah," Lexi started. "But we don't know where he is. We put a huge wrench in his plans. Maybe he realized he doesn't stand a chance."

"We don't know that," Tristan said. "The fact we haven't heard from him makes me nervous."

"I know, I know," Lexi sighed. "We'll just proceed with caution like we have been."

I shook my head. "I'm all for forgetting about Darien and going back to my boring life, but I can't help feeling like something is wrong."

"I know what you mean," Tristan said.

"Guys," Lexi whined. "Can we please just enjoy our time while we can? We'll figure everything else out later."

"You can't be so reckless," Tristan said.

Lexi's mouth tightened. "Right now, it's my birthday week and I say we go shopping today and have fun."

I laughed. "I'm down for some fun."

Tristan just shook his head.

We pulled into the parking lot at the mall, and it was surprisingly busy for the middle of the week. Tristan parked his Camaro and we pried ourselves out of the car.

"I still think we should have taken my Mustang," I said, already missing its metallic blue finish.

"I still think we should have teleported," Lexi said. "But *someone* wanted to blend in." She shot a glare at Tristan.

"Why?" Tristan asked me, ignoring Lexi. "Your Mustang's not any bigger."

"Yeah, but it's better," I said, slamming the door as I finally squeezed myself out of the back seat.

"Hey, easy on the door," Tristan said as he locked the car. "And it's not better."

I rolled my eyes, and Lexi chuckled.

The sliding glass doors opened for us as we walked into the department store and the air conditioning wrapped around us.

"Where do you want to go first?" I asked Lexi.

She just smiled and said, "Follow me."

We did. Lexi walked ahead while Tristan and I hung back.

"It's nice of you to come," I said. "I don't care much for shopping, so I can only imagine how annoying this will be for you."

"I don't mind, I'm here to watch over you, so wherever you go, I go."

"That's only borderline creepy," I said smiling.

Tristan shrugged.

Lexi led us to a store that was meant for teenagers rather than women. I snorted.

"What?" Lexi asked innocently.

"You seriously think you'll find something nice enough here?" I retorted.

"Not nice, sexy, remember?"

"Right, yeah, sexy." This was not going to end well. I followed Lexi as she walked around the store, picking up one item, studying and then placing it back on the rack before picking up another.

"You try this on," Lexi said, holding up a small piece of stretchy fabric.

"What the hell is that?" I asked.

"A dress," Lexi said as if this was obvious.

"Where's the rest of it?"

"Ugh, Selena, can you please just try it on. It's stretchy; it'll fit."

"Like hell," I mumbled, but I took the offending garment from her.

"I'll try this on," Lexi held a white mini-skirt and a blouse with a dangerously low neckline.

"Are we celebrating a birthday or hanging out on a corner?" I asked.

Tristan chuckled.

"Selena," Lexi said, and with that one word I knew to zip-it and try on the dress to make her happy.

"Fine, let's go to the fitting rooms." I led the way and Lexi eagerly followed. Tristan walked slowly behind us and stopped at the entrance of the changing room area. I walked into a room and latched the wooden door behind me. I undressed quickly and huffed and squeezed into the tiny red dress. Lexi was right; it did fit, and even though it sealed itself to my skin, I was able to appreciate that it did look sexy. It was short though… really short. Like wrapping around my ass and then ending short.

"I don't know about this," I called over the stall.

"Show me," Lexi called back and I heard her unlock her room door. I poked my head out and saw Lexi standing in her outfit.

"I don't think I like this," she said, checking herself out in the three-way mirror.

"I've seen you in better," I agreed. "Let's try another store."

"Wait, you have to let me see that dress on you," Lexi said. I bit my lip and spotted Tristan leaning against the wall looking at us.

"No, I don't think so," I said.

"Please," Lexi said. "I'm so curious to see it."

I let out a groan and reluctantly stepped out, pulling the dress down as I walked.

"Damn," Lexi said.

"I..." I started, then I looked at Tristan, knowing he would agree with me. "Isn't this too slutty?" I asked him. His eyes trailed over my body once, and he clenched his jaw. I felt the heat rise to my face, but I wasn't sure why.

"Yeah," he said gruffly.

"Oh, come on," Lexi said. "We want sexy, and this is damn sexy. Even you can't deny that, Tristan."

Tristan opened his mouth to respond, then closed it. He turned and left the room.

"See?" I asked. "I'm so changing."

"Fine," Lexi huffed.

A few minutes later we were back in our own clothes and walking out of the store.

"Can we go somewhere a little more age appropriate please?" I asked.

"Selena," Lexi said. "You make it sound like you're so old."

"I feel that way sometimes." I sighed.

Tristan remained silent, walking behind us a few steps. I felt awkward, like he was a bodyguard I couldn't socialize with. Lexi and I went to a few more stores before finding something we both liked. I paid for her outfit as her birthday gift since I knew I wouldn't find time to get her something else. Tristan never came into the change rooms again, and spoke only briefly when he spoke at all.

"Hey, can we pass by the bookstore?" I asked. I hadn't had time to read, let alone shop for any books, but I really missed it. Just walking in a book store would make me feel good.

"Sure," Lexi said as she led the way. We passed a line of clothing stores, a home décor store, and a few cell phone and hair accessory kiosks before we reached the book store. It was at the end of the mall with doors leading customers in from outside as well. The entrance we came through had glass doors and lights shining down on the books like a spotlight making the entire store look large and open.

I smiled in spite of myself as I crossed the threshold. There was something so tranquil about a book store. I remembered sitting on my dad's lap as he read me another one of his favorite books. His voice, so animated with the printed words, rang in my ears and my heart ached at the memory. Lexi forked away from me and toward the magazine stands, bringing me back to the present. Tristan followed me as I walked to the sci-fi and fantasy section, and stood by me as I scanned the shelves.

"You don't have to stay with me," I told Tristan. "I'm sure you can find The Rock's autobiography around here somewhere." Tristan told me once that it was his favorite book. I still wasn't sure if he was being honest about that or not, but I knew he would rather be in a different section than fantasy. Then again, he was reading the Brothers Grimm short stories, so who knew?

"I'm okay here," he said shortly.

I shrugged and kept perusing the titles. I lifted a black book off the shelf that caught my attention, and studied the art work. It was a drawing of a woman riding a horse with her sword drawn, as if she were in the midst of battle.

"Didn't anyone ever tell you not to judge a book by its cover?" Tristan asked.

"Oh, yeah, all the time. Only they weren't ever actually referring to books," I answered as I put the book back.

Tristan smiled and I felt relieved that he wasn't in his super bodyguard mode.

I lifted another book and read the synopsis on the back. "This one sounds good," I said. It was about a girl who could speak with the dead.

"Do you think you will actually have time to read?" Tristan asked.

"Maybe not, but I can always sneak in a few pages before bed. I just need something to escape into once in a while."

Tristan nodded, and we went to find Lexi. She stood in front of the magazines, holding *People* magazine and flipping through the pages.

"Are you going to buy that?" I asked her.

"Nah, pretty much finished reading through it anyway," she answered. "You ready?"

"Yep," I said holding up the book to show her.

After the bookstore, we decided to get some pizza for lunch. We weaved through the lunchtime throng and managed to find an unoccupied table in the food court.

I devoured my pepperoni pizza while Lexi nibbled her plain cheese slice. Tristan intermittently took bites of his meat lover's slice while scoping the area.

"Tristan, you should buy a nice outfit too," Lexi said, after we finished eating.

"No."

"Jeez," Lexi mumbled. "You'd think I was asking him to do a strip-tease."

Tristan glared at her. "You girls ready to go?" He asked.

"Yeah, I guess so," Lexi answered.

"It's still early," Tristan said. "We could fit in a training session." He looked at me and I groaned.

"What happened to a day off?" I asked.

"We shouldn't waste any time," Tristan answered. "If we can fit in training, we should."

"Damn," I mumbled. Lexi shot me an apologetic glance. We grabbed our bags and left the mall, reaching Tristan's house half an hour later.

"Wait," I protested before we got out of the car. "I need to change, can you take me home?"

"I have some work-out clothes for you," Tristan said.

"You do?" I asked surprised and saw that Lexi looked confused as well.

"Yes," he started, and then seeing our expressions quickly continued. "I didn't buy you anything, I just have some old clothes that would fit you."

"I live like, two minutes away," I said. "Or I could teleport there." I could never get sick of being able to pop in and out of any place I wanted to. Never mind the exhilaration of it.

"Just get out of the car," Tristan said. "I don't want to waste any more time." He opened his car door and gracefully stepped out of the car before closing it.

"Cranky, isn't he?" I whispered to Lexi. She studied Tristan and nodded her head like she knew something I didn't.

She unbuckled her seat belt and stepped out of the car, pulling her seat up so I could squeeze out too. Seeing my expression Lexi whispered to me. "Tristan is a man of action. He needs to know that he's being productive. He also needs to do something to get his mind off things and training with you will help him do that."

"What's bothering him so much that he has to train immediately?" I asked, and stepped out of the car.

Again, Lexi had a look on her face that said she knew the answer, but wasn't sure if she should say anything. She shrugged instead.

We walked into Tristan's house and he went to the bedroom. I remembered when the three of us had shared that room to stay safe from Darien and his followers. Tristan returned quickly with a t-shirt and shorts draped over his arm.

"Here," he said handing them to me.

I mumbled a thanks and went to the bathroom to change. I threw the t-shirt on, which was pretty baggy and then the shorts. They were training shorts with a draw string that I had to pull all the way to make them tight enough. I hoped they wouldn't fall off when I started fighting. I could tell they wouldn't fit Tristan now, since they just barely fit me. If I wore his current clothes I'd be swimming in them. I wondered why he kept these.

I walked out of the bathroom and Lexi chuckled, "From the slinky red dress to this?"

"I'm training, not going out," I said, trying to sound responsible, but I glared at her anyway.

"Okay, we're going to practice elemental spells today," Tristan instructed, opening a tattered book, and flipping through the worn pages. We had been practicing my elemental magic ever since we found out I could control and manifest each element. Most witches could control one or two, but some witches couldn't manifest them at all.

"What is that?" I asked.

"An old school textbook I found," Tristan said, still thumbing through the pages. "I forgot I had kept it all these years."

"Oh, man, I remember that one!" Lexi said, jumping beside Tristan and pulling the book from his hands.

"Hey," Tristan said, but Lexi ignored him. A smile crossed her face as she ran her hand over the cover. Tristan pulled the book away from Lexi and resumed his page turning.

"Anyways," he said as though the exchange never happened. "I found a section where they teach the basics of elemental magic. Not how to throw fireballs or icicles, but build fire, and create ice from the moisture in the air. I think if you learn to manifest the elements on a basic level, it will help you manifest them into weapons."

"But I already learned that."

"That's what you think." Tristan smiled. He handed me the book opened to a page about manipulating air.

"Alright," I said on a sigh and read the instructions. I held my hand out like the picture showed, and twisted my wrist. The book described it as the first step in feeling the air before being able to command it. The motion was supposed to cause wind around my hand, but nothing happened.

"Not as easy as it looks, is it?" Tristan said, crossing his arms over his chest smugly.

"This is dumb," I said. "How can I do this then?" I pulled in the air around me, and then pushed it toward Tristan, ruffling his hair and making him stumble back a step.

"Because," he said, smoothing out his hair. "You have the magical ability to control the element but not the fundamental technique. Your power is incredible, but you're painting a canvas with a roller. You need to learn how to fine tune your spells, to control them with precision. Sure you could just incinerate all your enemies, but why use a nuke when a single bullet to the brain could save a lot of time and energy?"

"So you're saying… what… that I should melt Darien's brain instead of blowing him up?" Though both ideas sounded extremely enjoyable.

Tristan nodded. "Exactly."

"That's gross," Lexi said, making a face. "His brains would probably ooze out of his nose. Yuck."

"Thanks for that visual, Lex." I said, making my own face.

"Okay," Tristan said. "This metaphor is getting away from us, but you get the point. I'll leave you to practice."

I nodded.

Tristan and Lexi left the room. I stood there a moment and took a deep breath. I practiced the instructions in the book, resisting the urge to throw it across the room. Stupid book. How could they expect kids to do this when I couldn't? I ran through each element, trying and retrying before getting some semblance of satisfaction.

"Alright, let's see what you've learned," Tristan said a while later, walking back into the room with Lexi on his heels.

I straightened up, facing Tristan.

"Okay, here goes." I twisted my wrist, the air funneled around it, creating a small breeze like it was supposed to.

"Good," Tristan said. I let out a sigh of relief.

"Do water next," Lexi said, hopping from one foot to the next.

I held my hand out, palm up, pulling in the moisture from the air until a drop of water formed. It hovered over my palm for a moment before I moved my hand and watched the drop hit the floor.

"Now let's see how your offensive spells take form, now that you have the basics down." Tristan fell right into his teaching mode. He stood across the room from me, and got into his fighting stance.

"Okay," I said, matching his stance. Tristan had the ability to control earth and air, so I knew what attacks to expect from him. At least I thought I did.

Tristan waved his arms and a gust of wind lifted me off my feet, throwing me backwards onto the floor. I shook it off and stood quickly. I retaliated with fire, forming it into small balls that I pelted at Tristan. I could feel the difference. The technique definitely helped me understand how to manipulate the element exactly the way I needed to. He deflected them easily with a swipe of his hand, some singeing the walls behind him. I crossed my arms over my chest and spread them open, sending a wave of water at Tristan. He tried to block it, but the water drenched him, soaking his clothes. His wet shirt clung to his muscular body, showing all the definition, and he swept his wet hair back with his hand. I was a split second too late to notice he had sent a whirlwind toward me. It lifted me off the floor and spun me twice before tossing me back to the tile.

"Focus, Selena," Tristan said, and I wondered if he knew the real reason I was distracted.

I bounced back up and shot a whirlwind back at him, trying to aim just at his chest but it went wide, throwing Tristan off balance. He stumbled a few steps, throwing his arms out for support, but didn't fall. I shot fireballs at him, trying to hone my skills and aim just at his arm, but I shanked it, missing Tristan completely. I growled in frustration.

Tristan swept his arms open, pushing me backward.

I teleported from my spot across the room and landed right in front of him, catching him off guard, and punched him in the stomach. He buckled over, but righted himself quickly and flung me away with a gust of air. I maintained my balance and got back into my fighting stance, but Tristan was laughing.

"That was good," he admitted.

I couldn't help but smile.

It continued on like this for an hour, attacking and deflecting, sending and blocking magic, until I was drained.

"That's enough for today," Tristan said, and I could swear he was *almost* breathless.

"Fine by me," I said. "I'll wash your clothes and give them back."

Tristan studied me in his clothes and nodded, "I'll keep them here in case you ever need them again."

I looked at the damage we had caused to Tristan's house and swept my hand across the room.

Good as new.

2. DANCE TILL YOU DROP

"So I decided that we should go out dancing for my birthday," Lexi said, bouncing excitedly on the couch beside me. I couldn't say that I was surprised that she wanted to go dancing. Why else would we have to buy sexy outfits? The last three days had flown by in a blur of training, and I was wiped out. I was too tired to share her enthusiasm, and I wasn't really in the mood to go dancing, but it was her birthday.

"Sounds like a plan," I said. "So now you're just as old as I am."

"Nope. You still have those 2 months on me."

I snarled at her. I couldn't win. Lexi chuckled. I leaned back on the couch and took advantage of the down time.

We had worked all morning on moving objects and trying to use my emotions to control them.

Blah, blah, blah.

I was actually glad we were celebrating Lexi's birthday; it would be a nice break from all the crazy magic training.

"Oh, I think I will invite Tristan along too," Lexi said absently. My stomach flipped, Tristan still made me nervous.

"Are you sure? We can keep it a girls' night," I encouraged.

"Well he's going to come anyway, so either he lurks in the shadows or he has fun with us. I feel bad for him, he needs a little fun."

I sighed, and then I felt guilty; it's not his fault I couldn't seem to keep my crush in check. Lexi looked at me then. "Not to mention he's really hot, so it would be nice to have him around. You know, make the other guys jealous?" She studied my face for any reaction, but I didn't give her one. She already knew how I felt about Tristan... well, that I had some sort of crush on him at least. She had no idea that he kissed me, and I wasn't going to tell her. I didn't think it meant anything to him anyway.

"Yeah, or he'll just scare them all away," I said.

Lexi laughed, but I could tell she wasn't buying my aloof act.

There was a knock on the door, and she bounced up to get it. She really had way too much energy. I wondered if I was like that before the 'training till death' madness introduced itself to my life.

"That must be him, early as always." Lexi opened the door, and sure enough, Tristan stood outside wearing aviator sunglasses, dark blue jeans and a white t-shirt that showed off his muscles. His hair was stylishly shaggy as usual. I groaned under my breath. Why did he always have to look so good? I looked down at my black tank top and jogging pants and shrugged. I was having a hard time maintaining my looks lately.

"So, Selena and I are going out dancing tonight for my birthday, and I would love it if you would come!"

Tristan made a confused face, then quickly recovered. "No, that's okay. Thanks though."

"Oh come on! You know you would have a great time," Lexi pushed.

"I don't dance."

"Who cares? Just have a drink and hang out, that's all."

Tristan looked at me for my opinion of the idea.

"Sure, it could be fun," I said, trying to look like it didn't affect me one way or the other.

Tristan let out a breath. "Fine, but if anybody tries to get me to dance I'm gone. Deal?"

Lexi laughed and I nodded my head. It made me curious to see how bad a dancer he could possibly be. I wasn't sure if I was happy or scared that Tristan was coming. Maybe I could just avoid him and let Lexi keep him entertained.

"Alright, let's get your training started," Tristan said, observing my comfortable position on the couch. I groaned.

"We're going dancing tonight. Can't that be my exercise? I mean I won't be able to move at all if I train today." I gave him my best sad face and watched his expression soften.

"No. Come on, get moving." Tristan stood with his arms crossed over his chest. "No one will give you a chance to take a break when they want you dead."

"Come on, Tristan," Lexi protested on my behalf. "Give her a break." I could see Tristan's jaw working.

"Lexi, can I speak to you in private please?" Tristan asked through clenched teeth. They went closer to the front door and spoke in whispers, so I couldn't hear anything. Whatever. I wondered why they didn't use telepathy to have this conversation. If I could use telepathy, I'd never whisper again.

"Fine," I heard him say, and then he walked out the front door.

"What was that all about?" I asked, worried Lexi would get in trouble.

"He just wants to make sure you can protect yourself."

"I know, but that's why I have you guys, right?"

Lexi looked at her hands, "Yes, you have us, but if something ever happened to us, you would be on your own. We know what you're capable of, but he still needs to know he's doing his part to make you strong enough to take care of yourself. Just in case..." She let the sentence hang.

"Okay, I get it. I will work twice as hard tomorrow to make up for today, okay?"

Lexi smiled. "Sounds good to me, but this is Tristan's department, so you'll have to take it up with him later."

Great, I was definitely not looking forward to that. Lexi walked toward the door. "Look, I'm going to head out, so you get some rest and conserve your energy for tonight. We will be back around 10:30, so be ready!" She yelled over her shoulder as she walked out.

I spread myself out on the couch and tried to relax. My stomach kept lurching every time I thought about Tristan coming out with us, and I was getting annoyed. Yes, he was good-looking... okay, great-looking, and he was nice for the most part, and strong but he obviously wasn't pursuing me, so there was no point in wasting my time. Right? I still couldn't seem to keep him out of my head though, and the memory of him kissing me fluttered to the forefront of my mind.

I punched the back of the couch out of frustration, and flipped over to my side. Nothing shook this time, thankfully. I forced all thoughts of Tristan out of my head and was finally able to relax. After a few minutes I was fast asleep.

I was back at the Aracali ruins, a beautifully haunting place that Tristan took me to recently. I was alone this time, and stood in front of the blue tree, studying its leafless branches as they reached toward the sky. The sunlight shimmered around it, and reflected off the magically-infused stones, throwing rainbows across the clearing. As I stood in the center of the ruins, the tree began to shimmer. Small, white flowers blossomed to life on the branches, quickly filling the empty space until the tree was full of them. The entire top half of the tree was now white, in beautiful contrast to its sapphire blue trunk.

I stepped forward to touch the white flower. As my fingers grazed the velvet petals, the flower turned black, and suddenly all of the blossoms withered into blackness and fell off the tree like ash. Death travelled down the branches into the trunk turning the mystically blue tree completely black as well. I gasped and took a step back from the now lifeless tree, as the light began to fade. I looked up to see a black shadow creeping across the sun. I shielded my eyes from the eclipse until the shadow completely blotted out the light. I stood in darkness and began to cry.

"Selena! Are you in there?" I heard someone call vaguely. A heavy knock followed, forcing me to open my eyes. I tried to get my bearings, but I felt exhausted for some reason. "Selena, you better not be sleeping in there!" Another set of knocks. I sat up and rubbed my eyes. Lexi was suddenly in front of me. Well at least she tried knocking first.

"Why aren't you ready?" Lexi yelled, looking me over.

"Huh?"

"It's ten o'clock, hello! Did you forget my birthday party?"

"Ten? What— I just fell asleep after you left like 5 minutes ago."

"Try eight hours ago. What's wrong? Are you sick?"

"No— I, I'm sorry, I have no idea what happened. I just feel so tired. Give me a minute." Lexi's face was full of concern now. Only then did I notice that she was wearing the short sparkly silver halter dress I bought her and heels to match. Her jewelry was simple and silver as well, and her hair was in her perfect pixie spikes. Her pink streak of hair was the only major color in her whole outfit, she almost looked angelic. I was going to have to put in a lot of effort to compare to that.

"Okay, go get ready. Tristan will be here in half an hour, so hurry up." I wobbled to the bathroom and washed up. I only had half an hour to get ready. How did that happen? I ran a brush through my hair, letting it fall straight down my back and threw on the tight black dress I bought. It had a square neckline and clung to every curve of my newly toned body.

I did a quick make-up job and threw on some gloss, grabbed a pair of earrings and gave myself a once over. I looked pretty good considering I still had 10 minutes to spare before Tristan would arrive. I threw on my black pumps and made sure I had my I.D. and money handy.

After all that running around getting ready, I found my second wind.

"Lucky," Lexi said, sitting at the kitchen table, as I came out of my room. I saw that she had relaxed now that I was ready. I gave her a long overdue hug.

"Happy Birthday, Lex!" She giggled and hugged me back. I let go and sat down across the table from her. "So why is Tristan taking so long?" I asked, hoping Lexi wouldn't pick up on the disappointment in my voice. Lexi looked at me sidelong. Really, she didn't miss a thing.

"He had some stuff to take care of, but he'll be here soon. He's not the kind of guy who takes hours to get ready." She smiled. We sat waiting for a few minutes before Tristan finally knocked. I opened the door to see Tristan wearing jeans and a black dress shirt with the sleeves rolled up to his elbows and the top few buttons open, revealing just a peek of his flawless chest. His eyes widened just a touch when he saw me, but he made no other reaction to how I looked. Lexi popped up beside me smiling.

"Glad you came," she said enthusiastically.

Tristan smiled, "You ladies look beautiful," he said looking at me, then Lexi, then finally the floor. I locked up and we headed out.

We went to *Majestic*, and headed straight for the bar. The club was full of people, most on the dance floor, but quite a few were getting drinks. We had to weave our way through them to get to the bartender.

"What would you like for your birthday shot?" I asked Lexi. She bit her lip in contemplation.

"Gummy bear!" She yelled across to the bartender.

"Make that three," I added.

"Two," Tristan corrected. Lexi and I looked at him. "With everything going on right now, I think it would be best if at least one of us had their senses on alert. You two have fun. I'll hang out with you, but I'm here to protect, okay?" We nodded our heads in unison. He had a point, but still I felt a little disappointed. I really wanted to see what Tristan would be like if he relaxed and let loose. Lexi and I gulped our shots and headed toward the dance floor. Tristan leaned against the bar and stood guard.

"This sucks," I yelled to Lexi.

"What does? The music is awesome," she said dancing harder as if to prove her statement.

I shook my head. "No, I mean you invited Tristan to come out so he can have fun, but he's just watching. He's lurking but just in the open. Why won't he loosen up?"

"He takes his job very seriously. It's a wonder he came with us at all. Don't worry about him. Just have fun and who knows, he might join in later when he's finished scoping the area for the bad guys," she said raising her eyebrows.

"So that's what he's doing right now?" I asked looking at Tristan. Then I realized that although he was still and looking casual, his eyes were everywhere, subtly taking in everything around him. Accepting that Tristan would probably never come over to us, I shifted my attention to Lexi and danced.

"So, since I am 'your job,' does that mean you get paid?" I asked.

Lexi smiled. "It's more of a volunteer position, but Tristan and I both have trusts. There are a lot of witches who believed in the prophecy and donated to create a trust for your protectors, A.K.A. Tristan and I," she said with a beaming smile. "As far as money is concerned we're fine."

"That's really nice," I said. It made me feel a little better that they were being taken care of. Then again it made me feel like a legitimate job. Their duty. I shook off the thought and immersed myself in the music.

Bodies bumped and grinded around us, heat increasing as we all moved to the fast-paced beat. I was getting in the groove and looking around when I spotted a man checking me out. He was pretty cute, had sandy blond hair, blue eyes and white teeth that brought out his tan when he smiled. I guessed he was an Arizona native or visiting from California. I turned back to Lexi so he wouldn't think I was checking him out, even though I was. He was no Tristan, but he was probably more available, and definitely more interested. I looked up to see him weaving his way through the crowd, toward me, and wasn't sure what to do. He wore a dress shirt untucked over his jeans, the top two buttons undone, and the sleeves rolled up to his elbows, just like Tristan, only this guy didn't look half as good. I sighed. His friends stood behind him openly appreciating him for having the courage to approach a girl. They hung back, holding their beers, and talked to each other as they watched the show.

"Hi," he said as he reached us. Lexi looked from him to me and then to Tristan. Probably to make sure he was still on high alert for any threats. "I'm Chad." He held out his hand.

"Selena," I said, shaking it. He gently pulled me toward him.

"Dance with me?" He asked. I nodded. Chad was a pretty good dancer. He kept hold of my hand, pulling me in and then spinning me outward. I laughed as he twirled me back to him and then dipped me.

Lexi stood by, studying us.

"Do you come here often?" He asked, holding me close. I almost laughed at the cliché.

"Sometimes," I responded. His smile grew.

"So, do you live around here?" He asked leaning in close to my ear.

"Yeah, about twenty minutes away." As soon as I said the words, I realized it probably sounded like I was inviting him over. Thankfully, Lexi intervened.

"Chad was it?" She asked. He nodded with his surfer boy smile spread across his face and his eyes roamed over her body. "This is more of a girls' night so..." She let the sentence hang, hoping Chad would get the hint. He didn't. His smile broadened.

"Girls' night, huh? Well I can handle two girls." I rolled my eyes. He had been much cuter with his mouth shut. Lexi made a face.

"No, you can't, and no we don't want you to try. Go away," she said, turning her attention back to dancing as if he had already left. Chad looked a little shocked, but reco-vered quickly. He glanced at me then found someone he knew, or pretended to know.

"Hey man!" He yelled as he walked off. His friends laughed behind him. I felt bad for him, and slumped a bit in disappointment. I turned to see Tristan watching us and I felt a little embarrassed and even surprised to find guilt in my mix of emotions, though I wasn't sure why.

"What was that all about?" I asked Lexi.

"No point in wasting your time with goofballs like that. I was just being proactive." She smiled and continued dancing. I sighed, then decided to stop thinking about guys and just have a good time with Lexi. We danced for a while, taking breaks only to get more drinks. After about two hours, we were feeling pretty good, and Tristan was still leaning on the bar watching over us.

I was starting to feel the alcohol loosening me up, and then I suddenly felt tired, which surprised me after my eight-hour nap. Maybe Tristan was working me harder than I realized. I pushed myself to keep moving, hoping my energy would pick up with the motion. The music was blaring, and fog crept up from the floor and rose toward the ceiling. The lights were moving in time with the music, making everything look disjointed. The music became muffled, then cleared up again. My limbs suddenly felt very heavy, and I almost lost my footing. How much had I drunk? I felt my body lean back in search of a support to rest against and I found myself bumping into a very large, and very drunk man. He was taller than Tristan's 6'2" by a few inches and was built like a football player.

"Sorry," I said instinctively stepping back.

"Hey, sweetie," he slurred at me, standing uncomfortably close, his breath reeking of whiskey. I grimaced and turned away. I felt a hand pull at my arm, and I turned to see that the man had grabbed me. I would have jerked my arm away, but I couldn't seem to find the strength. I saw Tristan straighten up in my peripheral vision, but he didn't step closer. I assumed he knew I could handle myself with one drunk man. Unfortunately Tristan didn't know how weak I was feeling just then. Lexi stood, waiting for Tristan's move. I tried to move away but the man pulled me up against him and held me tightly, grinding against my body in a morbid dance. I couldn't move, I could barely squirm to try to wiggle my way out of his tight grip.

In a flash, Tristan was by my side pulling the man off me."Whaddyathink you're doin'?" The man slurred.

"I strongly suggest you walk away before you get hurt," Tristan said in a tone so frightening I had to look to see if it really came from him. The man's eyes widened and he took a step back, then he looked confused and turned away. Tristan turned to me with concern in his eyes and opened his mouth to say something. I saw something move behind him, and Tristan must have read my reaction because he turned in time to see the man leaping toward him.

Time seemed to slow down for a moment; the man seemed suspended in the air. Tristan moved out of the way just in time, so the man landed on the floor face first. He struggled to stand, but seemed satisfied when all he could manage was to sit up. Tristan wrapped his hand around the man's neck and held him a foot off the ground, as if the huge man were light as a feather. Fury blazed in his green eyes as the man tried to break free and get some air. Finally tiring of the lack of challenge, Tristan threw the man, and he soared across the dance floor, landing with a crash. He led Lexi and I outside before security could come. We stepped into the warm air, and I took a deep breath to steady myself. "What the hell was that, Selena?" Tristan asked angrily. His reaction caught me off guard, and I looked to Lexi to see if she knew what he meant. Lexi was looking at me with the same disappointed look as Tristan.

"What? What did I do?" I asked, confusion written all over my face. "Nothing! That's the point. All of our training and you couldn't push one drunk guy off you?" Tristan grabbed my arms and made me face him. "What's wrong?"

I felt whatever energy I had left drain away from me, and I found myself leaning into Tristan's grip to keep myself up.

"I... I don't know. I just feel so tired. Maybe it was something I drank," I spoke slowly, the words swimming around my head just out of reach. I couldn't hold myself up anymore, black shadows played around the corners of my vision, threatening to consume me. I fell forward and Tristan caught me before I hit the ground.

"Oh my God. Tristan, what's going on?" I heard Lexi ask, panic evident in her voice.

"I don't know." Tristan's voice seemed muffled and distant. I could vaguely feel his arms around me, and wished I were more alert so I could enjoy the feeling. I looked up to see Tristan's green eyes inches from my face, studying me. He looked scared. I felt him lift me off the ground, and then everything went black.

3. MIND GAMES

I woke up in my bed, the sun streaming through my open blinds warmed my sheets. I felt better, but something was off. I sat up, expecting to feel dizzy or faint, but I felt fine. I got out of bed and the scent of coffee wafted toward me. Walking toward my kitchen I saw Lexi pouring coffee into a mug and Tristan asleep on the couch.

"Hey," I said to Lexi quietly so I wouldn't wake Tristan. Turned out he's a light sleeper; his eyes opened right away.

"Are you alright?" He asked with a little too much energy for someone who was just asleep. I nodded.

"I feel better, just a little off. I'm sorry I ruined your birthday, Lex."

Lexi smiled and handed me the mug.

"Are you kidding? It was awesome to see Tristan throw that guy around." She laughed. "Besides, all that matters is that you're okay. It looks like you're feeling better, thankfully. You had us worried there. Tristan insisted he stay up all night to make sure you were okay." She said, shooting a smile toward Tristan, who looked annoyed.

"Sorry I worried you. I hope you managed to get some rest."

"Don't worry about it," he said, glaring at Lexi. "It's not a big deal."

"Am I missing something?" I asked, confused. What were Lexi and Tristan up to? Lexi opened her mouth to speak, but Tristan beat her to it.

"No, there's nothing. Come, sit, you should rest," he said pointing to the seat across from him.

"I really feel fine," I said. "I rested well last night." But I sat down anyway.

"So what happened last night?" Lexi asked as she sat on the couch beside Tristan. I envied the comfort they had with each other. "Did you drink too much or…what?"

"I really don't know. It was like the life was sucked out of me."

"Lexi told me you slept through most of the day yesterday, right?" Tristan asked, and Lexi nodded. "I imagine it's connected somehow, since she wasn't drunk yesterday before we left. Maybe I have been working you too hard." He looked at me, only a hint of worry showed.

"I feel better now really. Let's just write yesterday off and start over," I said, sipping my coffee. Lexi and Tristan looked at one another and seemed to have a silent conversation. I rolled my eyes and felt left out again. I decided my coffee needed more cream and feeling particularly lazy just then, tried to open the fridge magically. I looked at the door and expected it to swoosh open, but nothing happened.

That was odd, maybe I was still sick. I shook my head and tried again. Still nothing.

"Huh," I said under my breath, but it wasn't as quiet as I thought.

"What?" Lexi asked.

"I'm not sure. I tried opening the fridge, but it didn't work."

"Try it again," Tristan said as a confused expression crossed his face. I turned and faced the fridge directly and willed it to open, but the door stayed closed.

"Are you sure you're feeling better?" Lexi asked softly, but there was a hint of worry in her tone.

"Yeah... I mean, I think so," I answered, but I did feel a little strange, like something was just not right. The silence in the room was heavy, and I was starting to worry when a shadow flashed in my peripheral. I gasped and spun around to see what it was, but there was nothing there.

"What is it?" Tristan asked, springing to his feet on high alert.

"I thought I saw something, but I guess not," I answered, still looking around.

"Maybe you should lie down," Lexi suggested, and before I could respond, another dark shadow flashed across my vision and I stood abruptly.

Suddenly there was a swarm of shadows and they merged into one large, black mass. I threw my hands over my head to protect myself as the blackness circled me and started closing in. Just as quickly, Tristan stood in front of me to protect me from the engulfing blackness.

"What's happening?" Lexi asked. "What do you see?"

"Nothing," Tristan growled.

Nothing? How could they not see this black hole ready to swallow me up?

"What do you mean?" Lexi asked.

"Just because we don't see it, doesn't mean it's not there," Tristan answered. The shadows swarmed round and round, faster and faster until I felt the air get sucked out of my lungs. I fell to my knees, and Tristan spun around and knelt in front of me. The wind caused by the spinning darkness lifted my hair, and then intensified until I too was lifted from the floor. Lexi and Tristan stood unaffected and rooted to the floor as I rose higher in the circling air. The dark forms closed in again, and this time they came so close I felt the cold inkiness wrap around me.

In my head I heard laughing and then that familiar, haunting voice.

Can't even stop this now can you? Darien said, and his laughter erupted and echoed through my mind, rattling my brain. Tristan jumped up and grabbed my ankle, pulling me down, but the blackness held me up, and thickened until all I saw was black.

When I was finally able to see again, I was laying on the floor with Tristan and Lexi hovering over me.

"Selena," Tristan said, "Are you alright?"

"What happened?" I asked as I sat up. I looked around my apartment, but saw nothing. The shadows were gone.

"You tell us," Tristan said.

"There were these black… things, shadows or something. They were everywhere. Didn't you see them?" I asked.

"No," Lexi answered.

"It was Darien," I said. "He said I couldn't even stop those things and laughed." I shook my head.

Tristan's eyebrows pulled together in confusion.

"It was another vision, wasn't it?" I asked, remembering when Darien made me believe I was being attacked by bugs.

"No," Tristan said as he ran his hand through his hair. "It was real, Lexi and I just couldn't see or feel it. They were meant for you only."

"Great," I mumbled.

"How does he keep getting past the barrier?" Tristan asked.

"I have no idea," Lexi said. "But I'll re-seal the place again."

Tristan nodded, deep in thought.

"Are you hurt?" Lexi asked.

"I..." I paused and took a mental inventory. Everything seemed to be in place and pain free. "No, I'm fine, just freaked out."

Tristan squinted. "You looked scared, but I wasn't sure..."

"What, am I not allowed to show fear?" I asked annoyed.

"No, usually you show it very clearly," he said looking around my apartment. Then I understood his meaning. I hadn't shaken or broken anything like I normally would when I got scared.

"Well, I have been able to control the effect my emotions have on objects much better lately," I said.

Tristan didn't seem to notice. "I need to check into something." He walked toward the door. "Lexi, will you be alright watching Selena by yourself?"

"No, I've only been doing it my whole life." Her voice dripped with sarcasm, but Tristan was already out the door.

4. THE ROAD HOME
-TRISTAN-

I left the apartment hoping Lexi would take care of Selena while I was gone. If what I thought was happening was really happening, I needed to fix it right away. Back at my house, I showered and dressed, but wasted no other time leaving. As I drove away in my Camaro I shook my head at the thought of Selena apologizing for my lack of sleep; she had no idea. Selena suddenly appeared in my head, her long silky hair, her golden tan skin, and those sapphire blue eyes that seemed to hold the secrets of the universe.

I shook my head. What was I doing? I could not, and would not, have feelings for Selena. She was my charge, the one I had to protect. If I didn't focus on what I had to do, she may never be the same, or worse, she could get killed.

I focused my thoughts, determined to find a solution rather than think of a woman I couldn't have. I needed to concentrate on getting to the Hidden City.

The Hidden City is the one place where witches could be themselves, and where they could find different or rare ingredients for spells, as well as shops selling items only our people could use. It also contained the largest library of books relating to our magic and abilities. It was called the Hidden City because only those with magical talent could find it.

One of the gateways is through Las Vegas; humans have no idea the secrets Vegas really keeps. Of course, there are portals all around the world since there are witches everywhere, and not all of them can teleport. I would have teleported to Vegas, but I needed the drive to clear my head and to feel the distance grow between me and Selena. I also needed time to figure out what I would need and where exactly I would find it. Besides, there is no way to teleport into the Hidden City, only close by. To gain entrance was a whole other matter.

I called Lachlan during my four hour drive to tell him I would be in town. I thought I might need his and Geni's help. I parked just off the strip and walked the rest of the way. It was midafternoon, the sun beginning its descent. Despite the weather, people crowded the sidewalks, many wearing minimal clothing. A group of men were laughing and trying to get the attention of a group of women. A man stood alone on a pedestal, painted entirely gold, as still as a statue. He changed his position which was the only way onlookers could tell he was human. How he didn't get heat stroke was a mystery to me.

People stood on the sidewalks handing out advertisements for escort services; others yelled that you could buy a bottle of water for a dollar. Ah, Vegas. I missed the energy here. Arizona was too calm and peaceful.

A young woman with short, brown hair cropped into a bob walked toward me and smiled, her pale skin gleaming beneath a short black dress. She kept eye contact as she passed. I looked away; I didn't have time for humans, especially when they in no way compared to- I stopped the thought, redirecting my attention to the task at hand. I needed to focus.

The Luxor loomed before me, a beautiful, sleek, glass pyramid that shot a beam of light into the sky at night. The tall pharaoh statue stood guard at the entrance. I walked in and felt instant relief, as the air conditioning cooled me down.

I walked across the marble floor and into the casino. Lights were shining and flashing everywhere. Patrons screamed; some from joy, others anger. I walked past a green Ferrari 599 Hy-Ker (for the environmentally friendly Ferrari driver) on display to tempt people to try and win it. I considered stealing it. Maybe later.

A tall blond wearing basically a napkin as a shirt and the shortest shorts I had ever seen walked confidently to me. I tried not to make eye contact, looking at her long legs instead.

"Hey," she said as she swept her hand across my chest. I stepped away from her touch and was amazed at her boldness. "Just because you're hot doesn't mean you have to be rude," she said as I walked away. I almost laughed. Women in Vegas were determined, like lionesses on the prowl.

Now to find that slot machine. I searched through the rows of shining, beeping, chirping, irritating machines, and let out a sigh of relief as I spotted the symbol only a witch could see. The swirl on the side of the machine shone iridescent under the bright casino lights; a beacon leading witches home. Unfortunately an old lady was spewing coins into it, a coiled cord stretched between its clip on her shirt, and the machine, where the card attached was inserted; she wasn't going anywhere for a while.

I paced impatiently for a few minutes which caught her attention. She looked me up and down, and then pulled her seat closer to the machine to protect it from my intruding gaze. I groaned and leaned back against the wall as I thought of a plan. I could go to the old casino on the outskirts of Vegas; there were a slew of magical passes there, but there were also tons of witches. I wasn't in the mood for the small talk that seemed to always ensue at those locations.

Besides, I didn't need to play on the machine, I just needed to use it for literally two seconds. "Excuse me?" I spoke to the old woman with as much warmth in my voice as I could muster. She looked at me and snarled.

"Go away! This is my machine. Go! Or I will call security!" She yelled, her hand hovering over the assistance call button. I smiled close-mouthed and lifted my hands in surrender.

"I'm sorry to bother you," I said and stepped away.

Damn it, this was going to be impossible!

So, I waited, but the wretched woman would not leave. I am sure it was to spite me, and of course that dreadful fear of leaving a machine, only to have someone else win on it right after. I tried to think of some spell I could use that would lure her away, but I couldn't force a human to do something against their will.

Then I thought of it, the one thing that would willingly make her move, even for just a moment. I moved behind the old woman discreetly and whispered a spell. The floor beside her shimmered then revealed a one hundred dollar bill. The old woman did a double take and leaned over to try and reach it without actually moving her ass off the chair.

Unbelievable.

Fortunately, it was too far away, and she was too scared someone else would grab it first. She looked around, no doubt for me, but I hid behind a row of machines out of her sight. She moved, and I quickly put a suction charm on the bill to stick to the ground. It worked. I hurried to the machine and placed my hand over the slot button. It was silver with a glowing green center, which was something different from the other machines that no human would ever notice.

I felt a tingling sensation under my fingers as the button responded to my magic. The button came off, and I palmed it. Within seconds another button appeared in its place for the next magic user. I moved away quickly, but the old woman saw me.

"Hey!" She yelled, still bent over the bill, the cord attached to the card in the machine stretched dangerously. She looked down where her hand was groping, but there was nothing there. I wish I could conjure money, unfortunately, or in this case fortunately, I could only conjure the illusion of money. She stood up abruptly and ran to her seat, with a look of confusion on her face. I laughed and walked back toward the lobby.

I got to the elevators and pushed the up button. Within seconds it opened, and thankfully no one was inside. I stepped in and waited for the doors to close. I knew there was a security camera in here somewhere, but there are spells in place to ensure humans don't see anything that could expose the Hidden City. Even if they could see me, they wouldn't be able to tell I was doing anything out of the ordinary. I lifted the button in my hand and placed it on the panel above the other buttons. It sealed in place, like it had always been there.

I pushed the button and the green center lit up. An audible surge of power signaled the elevator gaining momentum, raising me quickly above all the other floors. The elevator came to an abrupt stop, and the doors opened with a *ding*. The button attached to the panel dissolved into nothingness, leaving the panel as smooth and flawless as before. I walked out and found myself near the light beam that shot out from the top of the Luxor Pyramid into the night sky.

Atop a set of metal stairs, I found myself directly below the glowing lamp, and pressed my hand at the base. A metal hatch slid across the bottom of the light, moving the lamp out of the way to reveal a gap large enough for a man, but the light beam remained in place. I stood directly beneath it and leaped up.

The force of my powers combining with the portal through the light beam shot me through the air like a rocket. Before I could take a second breath, my feet touched ground. I stood in front of a large wooden door, intricately carved with the designs of witches, fairies and other magic users. I pressed my hand flat against the surface, and it opened slowly, showing the immense weight of the door. No physical force could open it, only magic. Behind it spanned the Hidden City. I was home.

5. JUST AS I SUSPECTED

The temperature was immensely cooler here, compared to Vegas, but it wasn't cold. I walked through the city and marveled at the green grass that was perfectly maintained. The sun was setting here, the trees full of life and leaves. The scenery was perfect. Amazing what magic could do.

My feet led the way down the path I had walked so often as a boy. I walked a longer way around a forest and through a cemetery, not wanting to pass the house I grew up in. I didn't want those memories right now. Instead, as I approached my old school, I was greeted by fonder memories. The old building stood two stories high, covered in brown and red bricks. It was a dark contrast to the colorful sky behind it. The numerous windows, which wrapped around the building each separated by three feet of brick, reflected the setting sun. School was out for summer, but the doors were always unlocked for visitors. I pulled the main door open and smiled when I heard the familiar squeak of the hinges, and the slamming of the push bar as it closed behind me. The hallway was exactly the same as I remembered it too, except it felt smaller. The door knobs that I used to stand on my tip toes to reach, were easily accessible to me now.

I could hear the ghostly echo of students running through the halls between classes, opening and closing lockers, practicing spells and laughing. I could smell the fragrance added to the polishing spell that would protect the floors and clean them the moment something foreign spilled on them. It smelled like lavender. I could see my friends encouraging me to try a contained explosion spell that was guaranteed to get me in trouble. I could see myself doing it. I could see the small windowless detention room.

I stopped in front of the office door, hoping against all hope that Derek would be there. I took a deep breath, turned the knob, and walked in.

The reception area was empty, which wasn't surprising since a greeting spell was put in its place.

"Welcome, Tristan Gabriel." A soft woman's voice filled the empty room. "Please have a seat. Someone will be with you momentarily."

I did as I was told, but it didn't last long. I was soon pacing.

"Tristan, my goodness how you've grown," a smiling Miss Laurel greeted me. She hugged me tightly, her plump body warm and soft as she tried to reach her short arms around me. Her short gray curls circled her round face, a style she hadn't changed since I'd known her. Of course I hadn't seen her in years, but she looked the same.

"How are you?" I asked, sincerely happy to see the woman.

"Oh well, you know how things are these days. Everyone's scared; they don't know if they're coming or going." She shook her head sadly.

"Has something happened recently?" I asked.

"Darien and his followers—the people are calling them the Wayward now—threatened to kill anyone who got in their way. At first people thought his threats were empty," she looked cautiously around and lowered her voice, "but then those who openly spoke out against him went missing, vanished from their beds in the night. Thankfully he's been in hiding for a few weeks, but who knows what he's up to?"

"What about the Charge? Do they have any leads?" I asked.

"Anytime they do, Darien is gone long before they get to him," she said with a frown.

"He can't hide forever. We'll take care of him soon enough." I hoped I wasn't lying. My bravado and fear warred within me. Many in the city believed in Selena and the prophecy, but there were some who thought it was all just a myth. The way things were going now, I couldn't blame any of those who doubted. "I'm actually here to see Mr. Russo." Derek Russo was my favorite teacher. He always pushed me to be better, train harder, and develop my powers. He was a well of knowledge, and just the person I needed to see.

Miss Laurel's eyes filled with tears, her face flushed and she shook her head.

"When? How?" I asked exasperated. It couldn't be true.

"The Wayward..." Miss Laurel choked out. She took a deep breath to steady herself. "Derek saw Darien around here a few weeks ago, heard he had something big planned. Some way to disprove the prophecy." She sniffled. "Derek went after him, following him to find his lair. He thought he might reveal his hideout to the Charge, or even a weakness, so people wouldn't have to fear him anymore. Or short of that, kill him. Derek believed in this city and our freedom. Whatever consequences he would face for his actions, he would have gladly faced if it meant we could live in peace again. He didn't get very far. One of Darien's followers must have found him snooping around and..." she shook her head, unable to finish the sentence. I hugged the older woman, trying to be gentle with her when all I really wanted to do was crush something.

"Do you know who?" I asked, trying to keep the anger and hurt from my tone.

Miss Laurel shook her head again. "I'm so sorry. I know he was important to you." She stepped away from me and wiped her eyes.

I nodded, swallowed hard and forced myself to focus on my task. "I needed to talk to him about binding spells. Do you know anything about them?"

"We don't teach that here. You know that, but maybe the library would have some reference on it."

"Are there any instructors here that would at least know something?" I pleaded.

"There are a few teachers in the lounge if you want to ask them, but I wouldn't get my hopes up. Elders would be the people to see."

I scoffed. That wasn't likely.

I thanked Miss Laurel for her help and headed to the lounge. There were three teachers there speaking in urgent whispers though I couldn't make out what they were saying. They quieted as they noticed me. All three of these teachers had at one point or another taught me.

"Well, look what the cat dragged in." Mr. Jenkins smiled. His dark hair was in disarray, his shirt was untucked, the top few buttons undone. With him stood Ms. Braden (don't dare call her Miss or Mrs.) Her short blonde hair lay flat on her head, tucked behind one ear. Her glasses hung on a chain around her neck as she tapped a pen nervously on the notepad in her other hand. She gave me a tight smile. Mr. Jordan seemed happier to see me, and more composed than the others. His blond hair was brushed neatly, his clothes tucked in all the right places, as he extended his hand to me. I shook it and greeted them all.

"What brings you here?" Mr. Jordan asked.

"Is everything alright with Selena?" Ms. Braden asked in a panic.

"I was hoping to find information on binding spells. Do any of you have any information on them?" I asked, avoiding Ms. Braden's question.

They all shook their heads 'no' and shattered my hopes with every left and right motion.

"Binding spells are forbidden, and so is teaching them," Mr. Jordan offered almost as an apology. "The Elders are the only ones that even really know how they work."

"Why do you need to know?" Ms. Braden's eyes narrowed.

"Just an idea I thought I could apply some of the properties of the spell to create. It was a long shot." I thanked them and left quickly. I didn't want to hang around and catch-up. The air was heavy with panic and tension about Darien and their hopes for Selena. The weight of it pressed down, smothering me.

I ran back down the hallway, suddenly needing fresh air. I swept through the main doors with a force that made them slam against the outside walls.

I took a deep breath to steady my nerves, trying to push aside all thoughts of my frazzled teachers and my dead mentor. I walked as far from the building as I could before stopping to regain my composure again.

"Tristan," I turned to see a tall, well-built man and a shorter woman coming my way. The man had short curly red hair, brown eyes and freckles scattered across his nose. The woman was fair, with long platinum blonde hair and green eyes.

"Genevieve, Lachlan, how are you?" I asked. I had almost forgotten I had called them. After everything I learned, I wish I hadn't, even though the positive energy of my old school mates threatened to dissipate the dark cloud hovering over my head. Genevieve gave me a quick tight hug, and Lachlan shook my hand. I hadn't seen them since they helped us kill Crystal, Yuri and the other witches Darien had sent after us.

"Can't complain," Lachlan said. "How is Selena?" His Scottish accent accentuated some words. I shrugged.

"Yes, well she is…" I wanted to say beautiful, stubborn, strong, amazing, but I couldn't. This was ridiculous; I had to stop feeling anything other than responsibility for Selena. "She's doing as well as can be expected trying to learn so much so quickly." I didn't want to tell them about Selena's current state until I had more information.

"Well there's no one better than you and Lexi to teach her." Lachlan smiled.

"Thank you. Did you hear about Mr. Russo?" I asked. Lachlan and Genevieve exchanged glances.

"Rumors are spreading that Darien found a way to weaken Selena and that she would no longer fulfill the prophecy," Genevieve explained. She looked into my eyes, trying to see if it were true. After a few moments of silence, she continued, telling the part of the story that Miss Laurel had told me, that one of Darien's men killed Mr. Russo. "It was Theodore," Genevieve practically spat the name out. The name didn't mean anything to me, but I was glad I knew who was responsible. I would deal with him person-ally when the time came. "With so many who rebelled against Darien going missing, and this outright murder, witches aren't sure how to stand up to him." I couldn't tell if Genevieve was scared or angry. Probably both.

"Mr. Russo was and is my hero." I shook my head. "We should all be so brave. I wish I could have been there for him."

"Selena needs you more," Lachlan said. "Is she really alright?"

I knew Lachlan was fishing, hoping that the rumor wasn't true.

"Darien is a snake, and will have his followers say anything to scare us," I responded to appease Genevieve, and hoped I was right. If Selena has been compromised I would never forgive myself. I had placed several spells to protect her from any tampering, unless Darien found a way to break them, like he did with the house barrier. My breathing quickened. I needed to go and find out what was going on. I couldn't waste any more time there. "I'm sorry, I know I called you to meet me, but what I need to do next, I must do alone. Don't give in to the Wayward's lies." We shook hands, and I made my way back through the forest and East toward the library.

If this rumor was true, then my theory was probably right, but Darien lied most of the time. I wouldn't put it past him to have his followers start the rumor just to cause panic. I didn't want to worry until I confirmed it myself. I walked past the shopping center where my mom used to take me for ice cream and the bar where I had my first drink. I was caught in the memory when a voice screeched its way to me.

"Protection charms here! Sale today! Get peace of mind for yourself or a loved one!"

I looked over to see an old woman standing behind a table with trinkets and jewelry displayed. I almost kept walking until I saw the necklaces; something about the way the sunset shimmered on their sparkling surface drew me in.

"It's for protection against dark magic," The woman croaked when she saw where my attention was. "I charged the stones with the spell myself." Her gray hair stuck out in thin strands around her head, her wrinkled hands spread across the merchandise to display them. I looked at a few; one with a black stone set in a silver bracket, another with a ruby stone surrounded by diamonds. Then I picked up a necklace and admired it. It was a tear drop shaped Amethyst stone the size of a silver dollar, hanging from a silver chain that entwined all the way around. I ran my fingers across the stone and felt the magic pulsating through it. It was potent, the lady had not been lying. I saw Selena wearing it to protect her when I couldn't.

"How much do you want for this?" I asked, already taking out my wallet.

"Well a stone that size is quite rare, and the enchantment on it is even more so. Three fifty is my price."

I counted the twenties out into the lady's hand. She wrapped the necklace in soft white paper and placed it in a velvet box, which fit in my pocket. I continued on my way to the library, enjoying the crisp clean air. I walked a few minutes before I saw the towering building. It almost looked like a church with its brick structure, wooden doors and pointed rooftops.

I walked up the stairs leading to the front doors, and then thought of the time. I checked the doors, but they were locked; the library was closed. I cursed under my breath, and headed back toward the street. I would have to find a place to stay tonight.

"Tristan, is that you?" I heard a familiar woman's voice. I turned to see a woman with pale blue eyes and a soft smile that brought back memories. Stefania's black hair was shorter than the last time I saw her, only coming up to her collar bone now.

"How are you?" I asked. "How long has it been? Five years?" Our last encounter wasn't the most pleasant.

"I've been well. I finished college, I'm teaching now, and I'm engaged." She smiled and held out her hand, displaying a solitaire diamond ring on her finger. I tried to pretend that I cared, so I smiled back.

"Congratulations."

"How's Selena?" She asked, changing the subject. She was obviously annoyed that she didn't elicit the reaction out of me that she expected.

"She's great," I lied.

"Well I hope so. You held yourself back so long for her. You left me alone more than once anytime you heard Selena so much as stubbed her toe. Does she know?"

"Know what?" I asked defensively.

Stefania raised her eyebrow and gave me a knowing look. I clenched my jaw.

"I have to protect her, nothing more."

"Right." She shook her head. "It was nice seeing you again." She smiled and walked away.

I headed for the closest hotel in the city, still thinking about Stefania. If she could tell my feelings for Selena, could others tell too? I had been careful not to look at Selena too long, or get too close. Was all that for nothing? Then again, Selena knew I had some feelings for her, even though I told her they would never amount to anything. Then I reminded myself, I have only platonic feelings for Selena. I repeated that a few more times as I got to the hotel.

The clerk gave me a key for room number 12. The hotel was one floor, 14 units total. Most people here have someone to stay with, but there were a lot of visitors throughout the year. Lexi and I had to change our lifestyles completely to live near Selena, so we didn't invest in any property here. Our sole purpose was keeping her safe. In my room, I locked the door behind me. I found the light switch and clicked it on.

The room was gorgeous, which caught me off guard. After being in human hotels, I forgot how exquisite enchanted rooms could be. There was such a feeling of home to the place, enchantments of course.

The only room they had available was a suite, with a small dining room, living room, bedroom and bathroom. It was too big for one person, but I enjoyed it anyway. The furniture was polished wood, the bedding white, and there were fresh flowers in vases in every room which made the place smell of lilac and orchids. I lay on the soft bed and sank in, trying to relax and keep my worries about Selena at bay until I could confirm them, but it was difficult.

I sent Lexi a telepathic message to let her know where I was.

She responded with, *Do what you have to do. I have things covered here.*

I hoped she was right.

My stomach growled then, reminding me that I hadn't eaten anything all day. I had been so distracted with Selena's situation I hadn't allowed myself to feel hunger. I found the room service menu on the coffee table and pressed my finger to the items I wanted on the paper. A few minutes later, a tray appeared next to me.

I lifted the metal lid and found my club sandwich and fries lying on the plate. Only realizing how hungry I was when I devoured the food quickly and drank the soda before finally feeling full. Pacing the living room, I hated the feeling of being useless. I wished I could do more now, but knew I had to be patient.

Undressing and crawling into bed, I hoped sleep would take me soon and quiet my mind. I closed my eyes, and lay there for another two hours before finally falling asleep.

The next morning, I woke feeling rejuvenated and refreshed. I looked at the bedside clock and did a double take; it was almost noon. Damn sleeping charms. I jumped out of bed, washed up and went to the front desk. I returned the key to the clerk, paid and headed to the library. It wasn't a far walk this time. I climbed the steps to the large wooden doors and was relieved as they pushed open.

I walked into the large building and looked around. The foyer was large and circular with a mosaic design in the center of the room created with different shapes and colors of tiles. The floor around it was high-polished black stone. The walls of the foyer were also circular, portraying pictures of famous authors and previous librarians. Straight across the entryway was another large, wooden door that led to the library itself.

Walking through, I had forgotten how many books there were. The floor-to-ceiling shelves were fully stocked; almost all of the books were old and frayed, containing knowledge passed down through the generations. There were books with enchantments on them to display everything written in the pages like a movie. I read one before, or I guess I should say watched one. As each page was flipped the words would dissolve into the paper and beautifully drawn moving pictures would appear, the dialogue would shimmer on the bottom of the page as the characters said them. There were books that could only be opened by a blood relative of the author. Some sparkled and shimmered where they sat, drawing the eye, and easily making you forget what you were initially looking for. Others wiggled, almost whispering to you to pick them up and peruse their worn pages.

Large stone pillars stood impressively between the bookshelves, comfortable chairs placed in front of them, welcoming every reader to lose themselves here.

"Ah, young Tristan, what brings you by today?" I turned to see Mrs. Ledsmith, the librarian, standing behind me. She smiled, her grey hair pulled back in a bun on the top of her head, her glasses perched on the tip of her nose. She wore a knee-length grey dress with a white shawl over her shoulders. She had been the librarian here since before I was born. She was looking pretty good considering she was over 100 years old. I smiled back, remembering the numerous nights I came here after school, and the delicious sandwiches she would sneak to me.

"Mrs. Ledsmith, it's good to see you. I am actually looking for information on binding spells."

"Binding spells? Tell me you don't know anyone who would bind someone's powers! It's a violation; it goes against who we are."

I shook my head, "No, nothing like that."

"I hope not. A witch could die just by trying such a powerful spell. You know only Elders can successfully perform them, and that's only after it's been agreed upon in the courts."

"I know that, I just need some information about it."

Mrs. Ledsmith squinted her eyes. "Is everything okay with Selena, Tristan?" She asked. I nodded and smiled to reassure her. "Alright then, follow me."

She led me to the back corner of the library. The musty smell of books filled the air. Sunlight shone through the windows and exposed the disturbing amount of dust hovering around us. "This shelf is full of books that mention bindings. I hope you find what you're looking for." She gave my shoulder a tight squeeze and left.

I picked up a book, skimmed through it, but didn't find the information I needed. I placed it back on the shelf and picked up the next book.

I continued on like this for a few hours. None of the books detailed how to perform a binding spell, but some would mention the effects they had on a witch. I knew all too well how a binding spell worked, but I couldn't find anything I didn't already know. I was getting irritated with my lack of progress. I needed to find something, anything, to give me some hope.

"Tristan," Mrs. Ledsmith interrupted. I looked up from the book I was searching to see her standing above me. "I remembered an old book I had stored in the back room, but I'm not sure if it contains what you're looking for." She placed the book on the table. "I hope it helps."

"Thank you," I said. She smiled and left.

I looked at the old book with black silk ribbon binding it together, tempting me to open it. Feeling like I had nothing left to lose, I picked up the book and flipped through some of the pages before coming across something interesting. My heart sank in response, my theory was correct. The amount of information wasn't what I was hoping for, but it was better than nothing. I wasn't sure I could handle this... not again. I had to make sure this time things were different. I took the book to Mrs. Ledsmith.

She smiled and waved her hand over it. "It will re-appear back here in the library in four days. I suggest you get all the information you need as soon as possible." I knew that my name had just been entered in her log book along with the name of the book I checked out and the date.

"Thank you for finding this."

"Glad I could help."

I took the book and left. I had to get back to Selena. Now. I ran through the city to get back to the gates. I looked at all the doors that led to the portals. There was a white marble door that held the portal to Italy; a wooden black door contained the portal to China, a bright blue one that connected to the Bahamas, and many more surr-ounding me. I wasted no time finding the brown wooden door leading me back to Vegas. If you ask me, it should have had flashing lights all around it, but it wasn't my call.

I placed my hand flat against the door, and it creaked open to reveal the bright beam of light. I stepped out the door and fell, lightning fast back through the portal. I landed just below the light beam in the Luxor, back on the metal stairs. I ran down the steps and toward the elevator doors that had materialized when I came. They opened as soon as I reached them, and I impatiently paced as the elevator took me back down. I ran into the bathroom and as soon as I had the stall door locked, I teleported to my car. My body was used to the shrinking and expanding as I traveled through space. It didn't hurt, it was actually invigorating. I appeared in the front seat of my Camaro and was grateful that my windows were tinted so no one would notice. I drove to a deserted area.

"Lexi, where are you?" I asked mentally. In a flash my Camaro and I were gone.

6. CAN'T HIDE FROM BAD NEWS

-SELENA-

"Come on, Lexi! I am not getting this at all. I can't make anything move even when I get mad. Something is wrong," I said after many failed attempts at trying to move random objects with my mind.

"You can't give up that easily."

"You can't honestly tell me that you don't think something is off. I feel wrong, something is just not right. I should have been able to blow them off the table by this point."

Lexi let out a sigh. "I know. I just hate thinking negatively."

"I know, but it is what it is." I had been working for the past two days, trying to get my powers to kick in somehow but nothing had been working. I hadn't seen Tristan since he left me in Lexi's charge and I was starting to worry about him. I hated that I cared so much.

"Have you heard from Tristan?" I asked, though I was secretly grateful for the break in training his absence provided.

"No, but I'm sure he'll be around soon. He told me what he was thinking about your current situation, so it may take him some time to find what he's looking for."

"What is he looking for?"

"Wait 'til he gets back. Don't worry, just keep working."

"How can I not worry? Just tell me."

"I can't yet." Lexi answered apologetically. "I need more information from Tristan."

I huffed.

"Just try again," Lexi said.

"This is pointless!" I yelled, pacing my apartment. "I am just wasting time. I spend all day in here, and I need a break."

"You're right. You're like a caged animal right now. Hey, let's go to the lake. That should be a nice change of pace, don't you think?" I hated it when Lexi talked to me like she was appeasing a child.

"Fine." I crossed my arms over my chest and sulked. Lexi chuckled.

Lexi and I headed to the lake with nothing but towels, sun block and my book. Lexi's hot pink bikini straps peeked out from under her white, flower print sundress, as the wind from the open window blew through her short hair. I tightened my straps, making sure my gold bikini was secure under my black sundress. We didn't need anything else but the sun and the water. The lake was busy but not overly crowded. Families surrounded us, mothers running after their children. Random floating tubes dotted the water's surface. The smell of hotdogs and hamburgers filled the air. It was a beautiful day to be out.

The heat of the day enveloped us, and we were in need of some cooling off. We laid our towels on the ground, took off our dresses and jumped in. The water wrapped around my body instantly refreshing and invigorating me. It was warm overall but cool enough to keep us comfortable in the mid-day heat.

We swam for a while, enjoying the clear blue sky and the blinding sun. We splashed each other and raced like we did when we were kids (Lexi beat me two out of three times), and then we decided to tan and let the sun dry us off. Laying out on our towels, the sun's rays soaked through our skin.

"Hey, Lex?"

"Yeah," she answered, her eyes closed.

"Thanks for bringing me here. I really needed to get my mind off things."

"I know. I wish this could be more relaxing, that you weren't worried about anything though."

"Me too, but I'll take it anyway." I smiled to myself. We rolled onto our stomachs to tan our backs. Not long after, Lexi looked like she was sleeping, so I started reading my new book. I was quickly sucked into the story, glad that I had something to keep my mind busy so my thoughts didn't run errant. After a while, I flipped onto my back, and nudged Lexi to do the same so our tans could even out. I put my book down and closed my eyes.

"You call this protection?" I opened my eyes to see Tristan standing in front of us in a tank top and shorts. How long had he been standing there? My heart raced and I dug my nails into my palms as punishment. I would not like him. He looked over me quickly, then looked at Lexi. "You two are out in the open, eyes closed. I mean really I could've killed you both in less than a minute."

Lexi clenched her jaw. "Glad you could find us," she said bitterly.

"I thought you hadn't talked to him in a while," I commented, regretting it immediately. Last thing I wanted was Tristan knowing I was concerned about his where-abouts. Lexi looked at me and tapped the side of her head.

"He just asked and of course he can just teleport. Man I wish I could do that."

"Add it to your list," Tristan retorted. Lexi flicked her finger and a handful of sand whipped upward toward Tristan's face. He waved it away with his hand, and gave Lexi a scornful look. To anyone else it would have looked like the wind was acting up.

"Did you find what you were looking for?" She asked. Tristan nodded and his tough façade melted into sadness as he averted his gaze to the sand.

"Selena, I need to tell you something." He finally looked at me again, but made sure to just maintain eye contact. No wandering eyes for him. It made me feel insecure, but then I remembered my task to not like him, so I pushed it aside. Tristan knelt down at the end of my towel, forcing me to move my feet and sit up. It caught me off guard that he was getting this close without physical training as an excuse. It also made me realize that he was about to tell me something very important.

"Why do you look like somebody died?" I asked, trying unsuccessfully to break the tension. I don't know why I asked that of all questions, what if somebody *had* died? Crap. Tristan's face fell before he took a deep breath and looked right at me.

"The reason you were unreasonably tired the other day, and the reason your powers aren't working right now is because," he paused and looked at Lexi with such a sad expression, my heart melted and my panic rose.

"What? What is it? What's going on?" I asked impatiently.

"It appears that Darien has found a way to re-bind your powers. You haven't been able to use your powers because… you're human again."

My heart sank, and I had a sudden urge to cry. I thought I would be relieved, not having that insane responsibility on me anymore, but the truth was, I didn't want to be ordinary. My body and my soul felt the loss; I wasn't myself without my powers. "They started the spell and you slept from the draining of your powers. When you fainted, that was when the binding spell was completed."

"But that's illegal," Lexi said panicked. Tristan nodded his head.

"Do you really think Darien cares?" He asked.

"What's illegal?" I asked.

"You are not allowed to bind another witch's power. Only an Elder is, and only if the court agrees it's for everyone's best interest," Tristan said. "I am confident Darien didn't follow the proper channels."

"Court?" I asked.

"We have a law to abide by too," Tristan said. "If a witch abuses their powers, the Elders of the court can decide to bind them. That is the only way it is legal. They are the head of our government, the judge and jury." I remembered Lexi telling me about it briefly before.

"So, what do I do?" I asked in a whisper, scared that I would lose control and cry if I spoke any louder. The sympathy on Tristan's face was almost too much to bear, so I looked at Lexi for some relief. Her expression wasn't much better. She reached over and rubbed my arm gently in an effort to comfort me. Tristan watched her hand on my arm, and he swallowed hard. I thought I saw a flash of longing, but before I could think it through, it was gone. Just my imagination making me see what I wanted to see.

"When you couldn't open the fridge with your mind, I knew there was something directly wrong with your powers," Tristan said. "So I spent some time researching. It was hard to find exactly what I was looking for, but I came up with some stuff." He flipped through a book I didn't realize he had been holding. When he found the page he was looking for, he turned the book so it faced us.

It looked very old; the pages were thin and yellowed and the binding was a black ribbon that wove through the pages securing them together.

"What kind of book is this?" I asked, not reading the information contained in its pages.

"We have millions of books," Tristan started. "This one is specific for binding magic, but we have tons of books specializing in different spells and lore. A lot of information has been passed down through the generations because of these books."

"There's really that many spell books?" I asked.

"I don't think you realize how many of us there are out there, blending in with society, living like everyone else, but we are still our own civilization and need our history recorded. When it comes down to it, we will all have to pick a side, and we will have to fight," Tristan explained.

That was a lot of information I didn't really ask for. I was getting cranky.

"Not if I don't have any powers," I whispered. Tristan sighed and took my hands. I'm sure the shock was evident on my face, but he either didn't notice, or didn't care.

"Listen to me. We will find a way to undo the spell. Look." He let go of my hands, unfortunately, and lifted the book so I would read it.

There was a pen and ink drawing of a beautiful woman with long hair, wearing an 18th century style dress, with bell sleeves and bustled skirts. She stood with her arms held over her head, as lightning crackled above, her hair blowing in the wind. Below the drawing was the word *Veneficus*. I looked up at Tristan.

"It means witch, in Latin," he explained. I looked down and saw another drawing below the first one. It was the same witch but she looked thin and sick. There was a thick piece of material wrapped around her body, pinning her arms down to her sides, her eyes were sunken in, and her hair was thin, and fell limp. Below this drawing was the caption *Reus Veneficus*. "Roughly translated, it says bound witch," he whispered. I didn't need the translation. I felt like the woman in the picture. My hair wasn't falling out or anything, at least not yet, but I felt her weakness, and sadness.

"Wait. If Darien bound my powers, why would he send those shadows to scare me? I'm no longer a threat to him."

"But you can be again. Keep reading," Tristan answered.

"I can't read Latin," I said sarcastically. Tristan sighed.

"Keep studying the pictures then. I will translate."

There was a third picture of the woman standing with the binds around her, but there were tears in the fabric, and it was no longer binding her at her legs, the fabric unraveling from the bottom up. Her face looked better but she was still not fully recovered. It was easy to see that the binding was breaking. Below this picture was the word *Libertas*.

"Freedom," I said.

"I thought you didn't read Latin," Tristan said smiling.

"The only binding spells I know of have an expiration date," Lexi said. "Like the one Selena had placed on her originally. Does it say how to break the bind prematurely?" She asked over my shoulder. Tristan shook his head.

"No, but the picture shows that it can be broken."

"Yeah, but how do we know that it's not broken just because it wore off?" I asked feeling deflated.

"We don't. I just have a feeling that there is another way to conquer this." Tristan stared into my eyes. "I promise you, I will get you your powers back soon."

I swallowed, and nodded my head.

The heat of the midday sun was starting to sear into my flesh. I stood up and walked away from Lexi and Tristan and into the water. I dove in when I got deep enough and I did a few breast strokes underwater before resurfacing. My heart hurt, it literally hurt. I hated Darien for taking my powers, for taking away the biggest part of me. I think that was why Tristan was so sympathetic. A witch's power defines them, without powers they're... human. I don't know why I hated the word just then. I had been human my whole life after all, but just knowing I had power, being able to feel it course through me, made me feel whole, made me realize I had been missing something very important in my life. Now that I was far away enough from my protectors I allowed myself to cry.

7. THEORY

When I came back from the water, Lexi and Tristan were watching me, waiting to see if I was going to crack. They didn't know that I already had.

Lexi and I grabbed our towels and headed for the car. I sat silently in the passenger seat while Lexi drove. Tristan followed us home in his Camaro. I had this sinking feeling in my gut, a feeling of hopelessness, and I didn't know how to fix it.

Staring out my window, my eyes scanned the scenery, taking in the dull shades of green and brown the trees and mountains reflected. Even the scenery looked lifeless, a mirror image of what I was feeling. I didn't want to feel sorry for myself. I wanted to be stronger, not just for myself but for Tristan and Lexi too. My mind whirled, thinking of some way to get out of this situation so I could feel like myself again; not my mundane self, but the one who felt complete with power.

"How are you holding up?" Lexi asked, keeping her eyes on the road. When I didn't answer right away, she looked at me from the corner of her eye.

"How am I supposed to feel?" I asked, hoping to redirect her question away from my true feelings.

"Well, if it were me, I would probably go crazy. It's like missing a limb. Witches are only what their abilities allow them to be. It sounds weird, I know, like we can't survive without our powers, but it's kind of true. Not that we can't literally survive, but we just aren't ourselves. I don't know, I can't explain it." Lexi slouched.

"You don't have to," I said.

She shook her head. "I know, I guess I just want you to know that I think I understand what it's like. There are stories that we grow up on. We're told about bindings and how horrible they are as kids, you know? I mean, it's basically our boogey man. Not that we don't have real boogey men, because we do." She nodded at me for emphasis, then continued facing forward. "But that's how witch parents scare their kids into behaving... Bindings."

She shook her head as though the word had left behind a rotten taste.

"You know you're not helping, right?"

"I'm sorry," she said, and turned wide, sorrowful eyes on me for just a moment before returning to the road.

I knew what she meant though, and it was comforting to know that I wasn't overreacting. I nodded, and felt a sense of relief and purpose. I had to figure out a way to solve my own problems and I knew that Lexi and Tristan would do everything they could to help me.

"Listen. I never did thank you for watching over me all these years. I know it couldn't have been easy and I really appreciate it." I squeezed Lexi's hand and she squeezed back.

"Hey, my watching isn't over yet. You're stuck with me, honey." We both smiled.

"Okay, we need to think of a plan. I can't stay like this forever, right?" It was a rhetorical question but still, a part of me hoped Lexi would console me by agreeing. She didn't.

"We will do our best, babe, trust in that." Got to love her honesty; she won't even lie to me to make me feel better. Her words did help calm me a little though.

The rest of the ride was quiet, and before I knew it, we were pulling in front of Tristan's house.

"Please tell me I'm not training today," I whined. "I mean, what's the point?" I unfastened my seatbelt and opened the car door.

"No you're not training, we're just going to try and figure this out," Lexi said getting out of the car. Good, at least there was that. I pulled my sundress away from my wet bikini and scowled at the inconvenience of not changing. Tristan approached and waved his hand over my dress. A gust of wind swept through my clothes, drying them. He gave me a sad half-smile, strode in front of us and unlocked the door. I followed him inside, my heart sinking at the thought of my friends trying to help me regain my powers. I contemplated ways to relieve them of their burden. Maybe now that I didn't have any powers, they could move on and live their own lives. Maybe there was an upside to my binding.

"Now that Selena's powers are...well...you know, can Darien hurt her?" Lexi asked. Great, something else I needed to worry about. Why couldn't she keep this concern to herself instead of freaking me out too? I saw Tristan finger something in his pocket. As the fabric tightened around it, it looked like a small square object. A moment later, his hand moved away from his pocket, and he ran it through his hair, a look of frustration crossed his face.

"We will just have to make sure she's protected at all times," Tristan said. "They're calling them the Wayward now."

"Who's calling who what?" Lexi asked.

"Other witches are calling Darien and his followers the Wayward," Tristan said.

"Great," Lexi said. "Names tend to give groups like that more power."

"What is in a name?" I asked absently.

"Don't start quoting Shakespeare on me now," Tristan said and smiled.

I shrugged and sat on the couch trying not to focus on the negative thoughts that popped in my mind, I needed to stay positive and think clearly. Tristan sat on the floor in front of me, probably realizing the inconvenience of only having one couch. I made sure to sit on the end to make room for him, but Lexi sat beside me instead. I held back a sigh of disappointment, and took a deep breath.

"Okay, how do we find a way to get my powers back? I need to be able to defend myself against Darien, or the Wayward, I guess, and I can't do that without my powers."

Tristan looked up at me then.

"I am still trying to figure that out. Only thing I can think of is speaking to an Elder, I'm sure there are a few that would have some answers."

"Okay how do we find one?" I asked

"Finding them isn't the problem," Tristan said. "The thing is a lot of them feel that they are too important to be bothered, so it's hard finding one who would be willing to help us."

"Even with Selena's 'celebrity' status?" Lexi asked, a half smile spreading on one side of her face.

"That could be the one thing that would convince them," Tristan said. "It is for a good cause, but we can't tell people that Selena lost her powers. They would panic, and we don't want that if we can fix this." Tristan stood up and started pacing. He looked at me and amended his sentence, "We will fix this." He set his jaw and continued pacing.

"So, an Elder is... what? Just an old witch?"

Tristan chuckled at my question. My stomach fluttered at the sound. God I'm such a girl.

"They are the oldest living witches of our time," Tristan said. "They have a ton of knowledge and they are the ones who make decisions in our court. Not only do they decide who gets bound, they perform the ritual itself. They would know if there is any way to break it. At least I hope they would, assuming there is a way to break it rather than waiting for it to expire."

I knew I should feel uneasy with all the uncertainties of this spell, but I felt hope instead. Just knowing there were people out there who could potentially know how to help, made me feel better. My spirits were lifted to an unjustified level. I was almost happy. I looked up to see Tristan and Lexi staring at me.

"Are you seeing this too?" Lexi asked Tristan in a hushed voice. He simply nodded, a smile playing at the corner of his mouth. I looked at them, my curiosity must have been written all over my face because Lexi said smiling, "You're glowing."

"How can I glow without powers?" I asked as I stood up. All witches have auras, a light around them that glows brighter through their emotions. Mine was apparently blinding because of the amount of power I have... had. I sighed. I didn't think it would still show if my powers were bound.

"Your aura is all you," Lexi said. "Although it's an indication of how much power you may have, it's not your powers. It's beautiful." She didn't look directly at me, but above my head, like there was something flying around it. Her face glowed with awe and it threw me off. I had rarely seen her like that. The last time that happened was when I repaired all the damage at Genevieve's half-way house after Darien's army destroyed it.

I looked to Tristan to see his reaction, but he quickly looked away. I don't know why I kept trying to get some kind of attention from him; he didn't and wouldn't care about me that way. I got frustrated with my lack of self-control over my emotions, and walked to the other end of the room.

I needed to focus and I was having a hard time doing so with Tristan standing there in his beautiful way. I shook my head to clear it, when a thought came to mind.

"Wait. If my aura is all me, shouldn't my powers be too? No one should be able to just take them away, they are still there. What if I did some kind of meditation or something and just focused on unbinding myself?"

"Well, that sounds good in theory, but I seriously doubt it will work," Tristan commented.

"It wouldn't hurt to try though, right Tristan?" Lexi asked, all but nudging him to agree. I could see in her eyes that she didn't want him discouraging me in any way. Tristan cocked his eyebrow, obviously not agreeing with Lexi's method of positive reinforcement. He shrugged his shoulders instead. I don't understand why it bothered me that Tristan wasn't more supportive of my idea, even if it was weak.

I decided to give it a try anyway, like Lexi said, it couldn't hurt. While Lexi and Tristan seemed to be having one of their silent conversations, I slipped out through the patio door and shut it silently behind me. The bright sun wrapped its heat around me like a warm embrace, and I could feel my nerves calming.

I had never been in Tristan's backyard and I was surprised at what I saw. There was plush grass fenced in by a 6 foot high concrete wall. Along the edges of the lawn, almost leaning up against the wall were hundreds of different colored tulips, my favorite flower. There were colors I hadn't even known existed. I questioned how they were surviving in this heat, but quickly remembered the amazing possibilities of magic. I walked to some bright purple tulips and smelled their beautiful scent.

In the middle of the backyard was a large in-ground pool spanning at least 15 feet in length. Around the pool was a ring of concrete, separating the grass from the water. The clear blue liquid was inviting.

I put my feet in the water and felt the cool moisture surround them. I sat at the edge of the pool and relaxed, figuring this would be as good a place as any to see if my idea worked. I sat up straight, closed my eyes and took a deep breath. I focused on centering myself and remembering the feeling of my power when it used to course through me. I thought of my aura, and how Lexi said it glowed and imagined that I was glowing inside too.

I imagined the light breaking through any blockages of my magic. I held on to those thoughts and waited. Feeling the elements around me, I gave them silent acknowledgement; the water at my feet, the air around me, the fiery sun beating down against my skin, and the earth below me all made me feel complete. A sense of serenity fell upon me, and I felt a smile cross my face.

I wasn't sure how long I was out there before the sound of the patio door opening snapped me back to reality. I looked over to see Tristan walking toward me. He kicked off his shoes and sat beside me, putting his feet in the water as well. We sat in silence for a few minutes, Tristan watching the sky, me watching Tristan.

"Are you okay?" He asked finally.

"Yeah, just trying to be positive and figure out a way to solve my own problems," I answered with a little more attitude than I intended.

He looked straight ahead at the distant cacti speckled mountains peeking above the yard wall. A sad, knowing smile touched his lips, and just as I began to get frustrated, he sighed. "I'm not trying to be mean to you, you know," he said. "I don't ever want to lie to you. My purpose is to protect you, Selena, but not from the truth. I promised you I would get your powers back, but it won't be the way you think."

"I appreciate your honesty, but how do you know my way won't work?"

"I guess I don't know for sure; it's just more of a hunch." He shrugged his shoulders, but I felt there was something he was keeping from me. I knew better than to pry; Tristan didn't open up about anything. I looked away, staring at the tulips.

"I tried it anyway," I told him, and waited for another sigh or negative remark.

"Do you think it worked?" Tristan's voice was quiet, almost hopeful.

"I don't know. It made me feel better at least. I guess I should try to do something, right? Test it out?"

I saw a smile curl up the edges of his perfect mouth.

"Okay then. You look really fat in that bikini."

My eyes widened, and I am pretty sure my jaw actually dropped. I looked down at my sundress over my bikini and felt my blood boil and my heart sink at Tristan's harsh comment. I would like to think I was stronger than that, but to be honest, I valued Tristan's opinion way too much. I kept my eyes down. I didn't want Tristan to see how much he affected me.

"I hate to break it to you, but I don't think your meditation idea worked," he said after a few moments of awkward silence.

"Why's that?" I asked, keeping my voice low so it wouldn't crack. Then it dawned on me; I was so consumed by what Tristan said, I didn't stop to think why he said it. I shook my head feeling embarrassed at my irrational reaction. I really had to get over Tristan; he was seriously messing with my judgment.

As if to confirm my delayed thoughts, Tristan answered.

"Come on, I expected to get a rise out of you, but since nothing shook or blew up, either my comment didn't bother you or your powers are still bound."

"Then my powers are definitely still bound."

Tristan laughed softly then. "You should have seen your face. If you had full use of your powers, I think the pool would have erupted from the ground and shot 500 feet into the air." He laughed some more. I wanted to punch him.

"You couldn't have gotten me riled up some other way?" I asked hotly, irritated at the power he had over me, and that he had seen it up close.

"I honestly didn't think you would fall for it. You have no reason to be self-conscious and you know it, especially since I have been working you out so much." His smile remained on his face but he looked away.

I smiled at his compliment. It was the most attention I had gotten from him in a while. Then I realized what I had said. My powers were still bound. This sucked. I looked back at the beautiful tulips swaying gently in the breeze.

"Why tulips?" I asked, wanting to change the subject. Tristan's smile dimmed as he looked up into the clear blue sky. The sun reflecting off his skin gave him a surreal glow. He turned his eyes to me then, the sunlight glinting off the green and enhancing the yellow in them.

"I don't know. I guess I feel like they are just under-rated, almost forgotten."

I smiled at that. I knew exactly what he meant. "If you don't consider this your home, why bother planting them?" Tristan told me once that his house was a place for sleep and training, nothing more, which is why he had barely any furniture.

He shrugged.

"Just had a feeling that they would be seen by someone who would appreciate them." He stood up suddenly and walked back into his house. He closed the door behind him and wet foot prints on the concrete were the only evidence he had been there at all.

8. RUDE AWAKENING

I was sitting beneath a tree, my back against its rough bark. The night sky expanded in front of me, endless stars sparkling above me. The warm air blew gently through my hair and I took a deep breath, feeling completely at peace. I saw something move to my right and turned quickly to see what it was. Tristan stood there, watching me. After a moment he knelt beside me, and without a word, took my face in his hands. He gently kissed my jaw and my heart skipped a beat. His mouth moved closer to mine, just an inch away.

"Selena," a voice whispered. My eyes snapped open. I was in bed, darkness surrounding me. The beautiful images I had just seen now a haze. My heart sank when I realized it was just a dream, it wasn't real and never would be.

"Selena." I jerked up and flipped the switch on my bedside lamp. The bright light left spots in my vision for a moment before it cleared. Standing at my bedroom door was Tristan. I hoped my face wouldn't reveal my unease. If he had known what I had just been dreaming...I shut my eyes at the thought. "I'm sorry. I didn't mean to startle you. By the looks of your aura it seems you were having a nice dream, but we have to go," he whispered. I kept my eyes down, afraid he would know why my aura was glowing.

"Go where?" My voice was groggy from sleep. I cleared my throat, and looked down at my body. My tank was twisted awkwardly around my waist, and I adjusted it quickly. I ran my hand through my hair though I'm sure it didn't help much.

"We need to see if we can find an Elder to break the spell. We can't waste any more time sitting here. I'll give you a few minutes to get dressed and pack. I'm not sure how long we will be gone for, but just pack the necessities. We can always buy anything we need later."

I got out of bed after making sure my shorts were where they were supposed to be, and walked past Tristan.

"How did you get in?" I asked while rummaging through my closet for the smallest luggage I had. I knew

Lexi could come in anytime she wanted, but I didn't think Tristan could too.

"Magic." He smiled. My stomach dropped.

"Can anyone just come in here then? Like Darien?" I asked, hand stopped mid-air over the handle of my luggage.

"Not without a lot of effort. Lexi reinforced the spell, remember? Only she and I are able to come in here easily. Speaking of which, she should be here now," he said looking at his watch. I admired the tight grey t-shirt he wore over his blue jeans and my mind wandered. Stupid dream was going to make it so much harder to get over him. He looked up at me then, catching me mid-stare. I blinked and walked to the bathroom, shutting the door behind me. I washed my face and brushed my teeth. I was glad I had taken a shower just before bed so I wouldn't have to waste any time with that. I brushed through my hair and sighed at my reflection. I had no idea what time it was, but if my puffy eyes were any indication, I'd guess it was around 3:00 am.

I went to my bedroom to change. Tristan had made himself comfortable in my living room while I got ready. As quickly as possible I changed into jeans and a white tank. I grabbed as much as I could fit in my small bag and went to the living room where Tristan sat. I looked at the clock on my wall and saw that it was 3:07 am. Guess my puffy eyes were accurate after all.

"Where exactly are we going?"

"You'll see."

Just then Lexi walked through my front door.

"Hey! Are we all set?" She asked in her chipper voice.

"How do you always have so much energy?" I asked, wanting to drop my body onto the couch beside Tristan. I resisted though. If I sat down, I doubted I'd be able to get back up. Lexi laughed off my question. Tristan stood up and walked toward Lexi. She smiled excitedly, her only baggage was a back pack she wore. Her pink t-shirt over her jean shorts brought out the streak in her hair.

"Ready?" Tristan asked her, holding her elbow gently. I envied her elbow. She nodded and smiled.

"See you in a minute, Selena," she said in a tone that was much too lively for this time of night. I looked at Tristan and Lexi and my breath caught when I saw a bright light shimmer around them and then explode in a puff of white smoke. Just like that, they were gone. A moment later Tristan materialized in front of me.

"Where's Lexi?" I asked, still in awe.

"I dropped her off at the site so she could scope it out, make sure it's safe. We figured it would be easier to go unnoticed if we left in the middle of the night. I'm waiting for her to give me the all clear," he said, tapping his head.

"The site?" This all sounded so military. Tristan chuckled, and then stopped abruptly, obviously listening to something I couldn't hear.

"Okay, hang on tight." He wrapped his hand tightly around my waist and looked beside me. "Hold your luggage too," he instructed. I had been so distracted by his arm around me that I couldn't think for a moment. I clasped the handle of my luggage with my right hand and squeezed Tristan's arm tightly with my left. I had teleported before, but I found myself a little anxious. "Just breathe," Tristan whispered in my ear, and then it started. A slight feeling of pressure and twisting and then it was over just as quickly. It was exhilarating.

"That never gets old," I said as my surroundings came into focus. We were in an enclosed parking lot. A few cars were scattered, leaving most of the spaces empty. Tristan led me outside and the sight was startling. At first all I saw were lights, it was almost blinding until I could put the images together; the tall buildings sandwiching the road in front of me, the flashing lights displaying hotel and casino names, the scattered flyers and advertisements all over the ground. Ah, Vegas.

"Bet you didn't think you would be teleported here, huh?" Lexi asked as she walked toward us.

"No. Why are we here exactly?"

"It's the closest gate to the Hidden City," Tristan explained.

"What?" I asked, remembering when Tristan mentioned that city to me before. I just thought it was some mythical place.

"The Hidden City is where most witches are from," Lexi answered. "We can go there for information, to get to our greatest libraries, or just to meet others like us."

"It's the only place where we can be ourselves, so many witches live and work there," Tristan added. "It's also the only place where we can find the Elders since it's where the courts are." He grabbed my luggage. "Come on, you'll see for yourself." He started walking toward the entrance of the Luxor, and Lexi and I followed. I processed the information, trying to imagine a place like that, but came up blank. Yep, this was weird.

"So is this… city in another dimension or something?" I asked curiously.

"No, it's still on Earth," Tristan said. "You just have to do a little maneuvering to get there. Only a witch can find it. Don't worry we're not going into outer space or anything," he reassured.

I shrugged my shoulders and looked down.

"Where's your bag?" I asked Tristan, only now realizing he hadn't been carrying anything of his own.

"I got a place set up for us there already, so my stuff is in our room," he answered over his shoulder. Our room? Would Lexi and I be sharing a room with Tristan again? I pushed aside my excitement and kept following. His pace quickened and I hurried to follow. I looked over at Lexi, who didn't seem to have any problem keeping up with him.

We walked into the main lobby of the Luxor, and I was surprised to see it almost empty. Most of the noise was coming from the casino itself. Tristan walked straight toward the noise without a break in his step; he had obviously been here many times before. Again, I quickened my pace to keep up, Lexi now also in front of me.

"Take her to the elevators," Tristan shouted to Lexi, and she grabbed my hand and pulled me in the opposite direction Tristan went. We walked passed black jack tables and roulette, all scattered with people who apparently didn't need sleep. Someone shouted in excitement and I looked around to see what the commotion was about, when Lexi pulled at my arm, dragging me toward the elevators.

"Have you been to the Hidden City before?" I asked Lexi as we stood next to the elevators.

She smiled, "I grew up there, but moved to Arizona when I met you."

"Do you visit often?"

"Sometimes, but it's been a while. You've been keeping me busy," she joked, and then straightened her posture. I turned to see Tristan striding toward us. He still had my luggage in his left hand, carrying it like it was weightless. I envied him his strength. He held something else tightly in his right hand and as he walked past me smiling I heard him say something. I wasn't sure exactly what but it sounded like 'easier than the last time.' It was interesting to see him look so happy; it didn't happen often.

Lexi and I followed Tristan and watched him press the up button for the elevator. A moment later the elevator doors dinged open, and the couple inside pulled away from each other in a failed attempt to make it look like they weren't just making out in the corner.

They walked out past us trying not to make eye contact. I heard Tristan laugh quietly, and resisted the urge to do the same. He held the door open, and I walked in the elevator after Lexi. Tristan made sure the doors were closed before he opened his hand and revealed a small silver disk with a green circle in the center.

He placed the disk on the panel and the light glowed green as he pressed it, as if it had been there the whole time. The elevator shot up so fast I lost my breath for a moment and I had to push myself up against the wall for support. We came to a stop and the elevator doors opened as if nothing out of the ordinary happened. As I stepped out, I saw we were under the Luxor light.

"Wow, I never thought I would see this in my life," I said under my breath.

"It's pretty cool, huh?" Tristan asked, studying my face. I smiled and he looked away at Lexi, who rolled her eyes. Weird... whatever it wasn't worth stressing over. Tristan was suddenly directly under the light and it shifted to create some kind of door. I was starting to get nervous, mainly because I had no idea what to expect from any of this. My imagination had a way of making my fear of the unknown unbearable.

"Wait. Shouldn't we give Selena a heads up on what to do?" Lexi asked.

That beautiful girl.

"Right, yeah you are going to jump into the light and we'll see you on the other side."

"What? What do you mean?" Could he be any more vague?

Tristan smiled and jumped up. He and my luggage were sucked up into the light beam and disappeared. I swallowed hard.

"Come on, it's easy," Lexi encouraged. "I'll be right behind you." I took a step up toward the light and then stopped.

"Do I need to use magic to make this work? Because, in case you forgot, I don't have any."

"You are a witch, even if you feel human right now, you're not. You'll be fine; just jump."

"I don't think I can do this. This is all so crazy!"

"I know it's a lot to take in especially since you are so new to magic in general, but the best way to learn sometimes is to just do it. I promise it won't hurt, you'll probably like it actually."

My heart rate quickened and I had the sudden feeling of anticipation I got when I was about to go on a roller coaster. I swallowed hard again and took a deep breath. I stepped up higher on the ladder and found myself directly below the light beam. Now that I was this close I wondered how the beam stayed in place when the light was moved. Huh, magic. All I had to do now was jump. Okay, jump.

I didn't.

"Just do it already! You think too much," Lexi yelled from behind me. She really did know me too well. I stood still and before I could think it to death, I jumped up. The light enveloped me and sucked me up into it. I shot up so fast I could feel my cheeks flapping. My stomach dropped at the feeling, and I was tempted to scream from the sensation, but before I could get my mouth open to shriek, my feet hit ground. How I was able to land feet first was beyond me. Magic defied the laws of physics and gravity apparently.

Tristan was there waiting and he steadied me as I almost lost my balance. My legs were a little too shaken from the trip to hold me up properly. Tristan kept his hand at the small of my back until I was able to stand on my own. I was too distracted to appreciate his touch.

"That was crazy," I said quietly.

Tristan nodded. "You get used to it."

Lexi popped up then with a huge grin on her face. "I can never get sick of that!"

Tristan turned and faced a huge wooden door. I had never seen anything so big; it was intimidating. He pressed his palms up against the wood and the door slowly pushed open.

"Selena," Tristan started in a soft voice. My heart trilled at the sound of my name. "Welcome to the Hidden City."

9. HIDDEN CITY

The Hidden City was beautiful. The temperature was perfect, even in the middle of the night. The moonlight shone brightly and reflected its light off the trees and grass, giving everything an unearthly glow. The stars sparkled more brightly than I ever thought possible and my breath caught at the sight. This place was amazing. We walked a few minutes and I realized Tristan was finally using the wheels and dragging my suitcase behind him.

"I can take that now. Thanks for bringing it with you." I reached my hand out to take the handle from him. He turned and cocked his head at me.

"Do you seriously think I would let you carry this? What kind of guy do you think I am?" He asked, hiding a smile.

"Not the chivalrous kind, but I'm learning," I said under my breath. He apparently heard it though and gave me a half smile, shaking his head. We continued on in silence, and it made me uncomfortable.

"Where are we going now?" I asked.

"The hotel, it's not far from here." Tristan walked straight ahead without breaking his stride.

"I love the hotels here," Lexi sighed. It was like she was under a spell.

"So how long has this place been here?" I asked, as my eyes took in my surroundings.

"As long as existence itself," Lexi answered.

"Witches were born and raised here, like humans any other place in the world," Tristan added. "Only, originally it was separate from the humans." As Tristan spoke, his voice took on an animated tone. "Legend has it that no one was able to travel to the human world until a psychic saw that his soul mate was a human woman. He also foresaw the way to connect the two worlds, and that's why all the doors were created. He was an innovator, and we're all better for it." He smiled.

"Did witches benefit from what humans had to offer, what they created?" I asked.

"Not really," Tristan answered.

"That's not entirely true," Lexi filled in, giving Tristan a stern look. "We can do pretty much everything with magic, like phones for example. Telepathic witches don't need them, but not all witches are telepathic, so phones helped there," Lexi rambled. "Or medicine. I mean we can heal most diseases and illnesses, but for more serious conditions and for those who can't heal, we need doctors and scientists in that area. There's also electricity, which we use even though we could cast a spell for lights and things like that. We use cell phones here too, but we use magic for the signal. So I would say sometimes we use human technology but we don't always have to."

I thought about my cell phone, turned off, in my bag. I already didn't feel the need to use it. I felt so connected with everything here. I thought more about what Lexi said, and felt slightly miffed.

"Witches should heal humans then! There are so many sick and dying from different illnesses every day." I was almost upset at the selfish use of the witches' powers. Think of how many people could be saved. I used to be able to heal, but I only used it for cuts and smaller things. The thought never even crossed my mind to try and heal a terminal illness.

"They do, Selena," Tristan said softly, "There's just not always enough witches with healing powers to go around. Not to mention the toll it takes. You saw what happened to Geni when she healed you."

I remembered how drained Genevieve had gotten from trying to heal my broken bones; she almost fainted. Imagine what would happen if she tried to heal a serious disease or even cancer. I supposed I could accept that answer. For now. "Okay, so if the psychic guy never had a vision, witches would never co-exist with humans? Why?" I asked.

"It's just a story, Selena, but to be honest, witches have always sought to preserve the magic bloodlines," Tristan said. "See, if a witch and a human reproduce, their off-spring is not guaranteed to have powers. It's a roll of the dice. So most witches want to guarantee their child will have magic abilities."

"Then how is it that my father, being human, was able to create me... the supposed super-witch?" I asked sarcastically.

"It was destiny." Tristan shrugged his shoulders as if this were the only answer needed.

We soon stopped in front of a large brick building. There was a white archway with gold carvings detailing the edges in the front. Past that was a circular drive way that wrapped around a statue of a toga clad woman pouring a jug of water into a well. I thought it was odd that she would be putting water in a well rather than taking it out. I studied the statue as we moved toward the front doors, and found an inscription on the base of it:

You must give to receive.

"It's kind of our motto," Lexi whispered to me. I nodded, and we approached the entrance doors. They were completely glass with a swirled golden handle. Tristan held the door open for Lexi and me to walk through. Once inside, Tristan took two large strides and was again in front of me, leading us toward the front desk.

Tristan exchanged a few words with the clerk before returning with the keys. They looked like typical metal house keys with a red tag dangling from the chain. He handed one to Lexi and kept one for himself. The key suddenly melted into their palms.

Um, okay.

"Are we in two separate rooms?" I asked, hoping my tone didn't give them any ideas as to the reason of my inquiry.

"No, we are going to stay together," Tristan answered. "It's better for your protection. It just makes sense for each protector to have a key, just in case." I tried to contain my excitement. Stupid dream.

"Don't I get a key?" I asked.

Tristan shifted uncomfortably.

"You need magic to conceal it," Lexi said. "It's part of the security here."

"Oh." I looked at my feet.

"Sorry," she said sadly.

In moments we were on an elevator. Our room was on the 4th floor, and as the elevator doors opened, they revealed a long hallway that stretched before us. The carpet was red and gold, the walls a creamy beige, decorated with oil paintings between the red room doors.

Thankfully our room was only three doors from the elevator, and a few feet from the stairwell; something I am sure Tristan arranged so we could get out quickly in an emergency. He held the doorknob for a moment, causing a whirring and clicking sound as the door unlocked. I gasped at the sight of the room.

There was a small hallway that led to a sitting area on one side and the bedroom on the other. The sitting area had a large black leather sofa set facing a flat screen T.V. that was mounted on the wall. Below the T.V. a fireplace was pressed in the wall. The elegant white mantle swooped decoratively around the large hearth. A glistening fire screen sat beautifully protecting the fire that blazed inside. In front of the couch was a black hardwood coffee table with a vase of flowers on it. I went to the bedroom next. There were two Queen sized beds beside each other, covered in the most beautiful gold comforter and sheets.

Between the beds was a white night stand with a lamp and phone on it. Two more oil paintings decorated these walls; one a depiction of a woman wearing a gold ball gown, sitting in a chair deeply engrossed in the book she held in her hand. Her golden hair swooped beautifully up, revealing her creamy skin. The other painting of a man, dressed in tights and a tail-coat pushing a woman on a tree swing in a beautiful garden, gave the entire room an air of elegance. Something smelled fantastic and I turned to see bouquets of flowers on the table leaning up against the wall behind me. I immediately felt at home. I saw a medium sized luggage beside one of the beds and remembered Tristan had set his stuff up already.

"If you had your stuff in here, why did you have to get a key from the clerk? Shouldn't you have had it already?" I wondered aloud.

"You are observant, aren't you?" Tristan said. "We have to return the keys every time we leave the hotel for protection reasons. Everything has become much stricter since the Wayward formed. So we aren't allowed to take it out of the hotel, or it sets off some kind of alarm." He looked at me speculatively then, no doubt wondering what else I would notice.

I took my luggage and unpacked the few items I had, hanging my clothes in the closet and putting my toiletries in the bathroom. I was finished and sitting on the edge of one of the beds within minutes. Tristan was finished almost as quickly, and then we were both sitting there, watching Lexi. She seemed to be able to fit an unrealistic amount of things in her back pack.

Every time I was sure she was finished, she would find something else in the bottom of the bag.

"I thought we were supposed to pack just the necessities," I commented, my eyebrows pulling together in confusion over the pile of clothes Lexi was going through. She shrugged and laughed it off. I looked at Tristan quizzically.

"She put a spell on her bag to hold more than it's physically able to."

"Damn, I wish I thought of that," I said, and then realized, even if I had, I didn't have any magic to use. My face fell, and my eyes unfocused on the carpet below my feet. I really hoped we could unbind my powers, I was feeling worse each passing moment without them.

"Alright, we should get some rest and start early in the morning," Tristan said. "The sooner we can get this done, the better for all of us. Selena, you still need more training with your powers."

"You're telling me. We still have to wait and see if I can even get my powers back at all." I stomped to the bathroom and changed into more comfortable clothes. When I came out, Tristan was already in one bed, so I went to the other and tucked myself in. Lexi was beside me a few minutes later. I tried to sleep, but the night's events were still so surreal and exciting. Not to mention the close proximity of Tristan, asleep just a few feet away from me. He was curled on his side, his back to me. If I reached out my arm, I could just touch the back of his head.

I rolled over on my side so I was facing him. My last conscious thought was of our kiss and what it felt like to run my fingers through his hair.

Morning came all too soon. I am not sure what I had been dreaming when Lexi shook me awake, but it left a feeling of unease behind. I really wished I was able to continue the dream I had been having about Tristan earlier.

"Wake up, sleepy head!" Lexi chirped in my ear. I groaned and rolled over on my stomach, pulling a pillow over my head. It was way too early for her energy.

"What time is it?" I mumbled.

"Hidden City time? 9:30. Arizona time? 7:30, well 7:31 now. Get up!"

"AM?"

"Obviously."

"No. I've been sleeping less than 4 hours. It's not normal. And apparently I'm jet-lagged."

"It's a two hour time difference, drama queen," Lexi said.

"Don't care," I mumbled. I started to relax again, and was inches from sleep, when the covers were pulled off me. I instinctively curled myself in a ball, but it wasn't even cold in the room. I spread out a little to get comfortable again, when the pillow was pulled off my head and I was suddenly being lifted off the bed.

"Lexi! What the hell?" I yelled and opened my eyes to see Tristan carrying me toward the bathroom. "Put me down," I ordered, though I knew I wasn't convincing. I didn't mind him carrying me one bit, but I didn't want him to know that. He put me down at the door of the bathroom.

"You have twenty minutes to get ready. Better hurry." He pushed me inside and closed the door. Wow. That was hot. I blinked. What the hell was I thinking? I really needed to get Tristan out of my head; it was detrimental to my health.

I took Tristan's order seriously though and hurried. I washed and dressed with two minutes to spare. I looked myself over in the mirror and was satisfied. This was as good as it was going to get. I was wearing my blue jeans and a black, v-neck, quarter sleeved shirt that was only a little too tight. I brushed through my hair and decided to leave it down.

I walked out of the bathroom and found Lexi and Tristan already dressed and waiting. Tristan looked me over for one brief instant before looking away. Lexi was wearing white jean shorts and a blue tank, and Tristan in his jeans and black tee. His shirt showed just the right amount of muscle, and I found myself raising my eyebrow in appreciation.

"Alright, now that you got me up, what are we going to do?" I asked, trying to look calm and casual instead of excited and flustered. I was hoping we could sight see a little bit while we were here. After all this was a magical city.

"We are going to the courts. The key right now is to find an Elder who can and will help us," Tristan answered, while putting a few small items in his pockets. I grabbed some money – did they take money here? - and I.D. just in case and put them in my own pockets. I wasn't sure how much walking would be involved so I didn't want to be carrying anything like a purse.

We left the hotel room and I realized the hotel itself looked much different in the daylight. There were so many windows I hadn't noticed before, and the natural light was beautiful. Tristan and Lexi dropped off their keys at the main desk, though I could tell they felt it was a great inconvenience not to have the keys on hand.

We walked outside and the temperature was the same as it had been when we arrived last night. The sun was shining, birds chirping, it was all so surreal, like a perfect little fairy tale village, except instead of shacks and people singing randomly, there were high rises, brick houses, corporate buildings, and even some really nice cars.

"Do a lot of witches live here?"

"There is actually a surprising number of witches in the world and yes, there are quite a few that live here," Lexi said. "The majority like to live with the humans, mainly because of the advantage they have there. It's cheating really, but whatever." She smiled.

"Do you guys wish you lived here?" I had to ask. I was so curious to know how much I had really ruined their lives by being at the center of this so-called prophecy.

"Well it has its perks that's for sure," Lexi answered. "I mean everyone can just be themselves here, and if you ever needed anything, magically speaking, you could find it all easily. But I like living with the humans too; it's not drastically different really."

"So, I didn't ruin your lives by forcing you to live near me?"

Tristan stopped walking so abruptly, I almost walked into him. He turned and looked at me.

"It is an honor to protect you. Anyone in our position would give this up," he swept his hand across the land around us, "and more to protect you." My heart raced at Tristan's words. "It is our job. It's what we're trained for," he added, squashing all the hopes I had a second ago. I was a job, and that was it. The sooner I came to terms with that fact, the better off I would be.

I saw Lexi shaking her head at Tristan in my peripheral, and turned to see why. She quickly stopped shaking her head, and started walking again.

I was hoping to get some sort of comfort, to feel like I hadn't taken them away from where they wanted to be, but I didn't get it. They said the right things I guess, I just didn't know if I believed them.

"What if I'm not the girl in the prophecy?" That question earned me another short stop from Tristan. This time I stepped on his foot. "Crap. Sorry. Can you stop doing that please?" I blurted out of frustration.

"One: Don't think that your tiny feet have any ability to hurt me. Two: You have to start believing in yourself. You will not be able to defeat Darien or anyone, powers or not, without believing you can. Got it?" He turned and started walking again without waiting for a response. Or he just assumed I got it. I let out a sigh and followed.

"My feet aren't tiny. They are proportionate to my body."

I heard Tristan laugh and couldn't help but smile. We walked the rest of the way in silence, only stopping when we reached a white single story building, with pillars encasing the entrance. The grandeur reminded me of the White House, the air of authority surrounding the building reinforcing the similarity.

"Ok, we don't want too many people knowing you're here. We don't know who to trust these days." Tristan said to me. "So don't speak unless you're spoken to, and try to be discreet. I will do my best to keep you out of the conversations too." He looked to Lexi then who nodded in agreement.

We walked through the front doors and I marveled at the lobby. The floors were white marble speckled with gold. The walls were white, but had a shine that made them look like they were some sort of stone as well. There was one long counter in the shape of a semi-circle that surrounded most of the circular lobby walls. There were around ten clerks waiting to help any visitors, and other people walking in and out of the lobby. It was actually pretty busy considering it was so early.

Tristan led us to one of the clerks; a woman with red hair pulled into a tight bun and a smile plastered on her face. Customer service? I think so. Her face was concealed with way too much make-up, and her blue blazer was fitted around a white dress shirt buttoned to her neck.

"How can I help you?" She asked in a high pitched voice.

"We need to speak to an Elder immediately," Tristan answered, chin up, keeping eye contact. The clerk waved her hand over a black leather-bound book.

"I'm sorry but the earliest opening is next Friday. Shall I set the appointment?"

"That's too late," Tristan hissed. "We need to see an Elder today." He poked his finger into the counter top.

"What makes you think you can just walk in and get an appointment with any Elders?" She asked, pressing her lips into a tight smile. Tristan sighed. I could tell he was trying to think of a way to convince her, without telling her about me. I could also see when he lost the battle. He stepped closer to the woman, keeping his voice low.

"It's about the prophecy."

The clerk's eyes widened, and then she looked over each one of us in turn. Her gaze lingered on me the longest, no doubt trying to remember the description of the girl in the prophecy.

"Well, I wish I could help you, but there are no Elders here today," the clerk said. "It's the day of the Bloomston festival, so they will all be enjoying the festivities. You could try to speak to one there, but I don't think they will be very receptive on their day off." She clasped her hands on the desk in front of her, hinting that there was nothing else she could help us with. I personally thought she helped enough. I couldn't help but feel giddy about going to a festival!

Tristan nodded, and mumbled a thanks. Leaving the court, I felt excited at the prospect of being able to find an Elder at the festival, but Lexi and Tristan didn't share my enthusiasm.

"This is good, right? We know where to find an Elder, and we get to check out the festival too. I don't see a down side," I said.

Lexi and Tristan exchanged a glance and then looked at me.

"That clerk was right," Lexi answered. "We won't be able to find anyone to help us today. We will have to come back tomorrow."

"Can we still go to the festival?" I didn't mean to sound like a child, but I really wanted to see what this place was all about.

"Well, we have nothing better to do," Lexi said, looking at Tristan for permission. He shrugged.

"Sure. But again, be discreet, and make sure you stay with us at all times."

Now I really felt like a kid.

The festival was only a few blocks away, and we heard it before we saw it. People crowded the streets, some in costumes, others just walking around looking at different things. There was a huge Ferris wheel, and some other rides that looked fun. I looked over at a boy being strapped into a cup-shaped seat. He seemed to be suspended in the air, no mechanism attached that I could see. The seated boy suddenly shot up into the air so high I lost sight of him. I craned my neck all the way up, but he was nowhere to be seen. I waited, and started to panic as the seconds ticked by. I finally let out a breath of relief as the boy plummeted – somehow safely – back to the ground, a huge grin plastered on his face. I decided to avoid that ride and stick with something safe like the Ferris wheel.

The whole street was reserved for small shops lined up in a row, each selling something different. There were trinkets, and jewelry, and house decorations. There were spell books and dress shops, and a henna stand, which seemed too mundane to be there.

I walked toward it and looked at the different designs. Then I understood. Each design had a magical attribute that would be applied to the wearer. There was a design for strength, and one for courage, love, health, and wealth. There were so many different designs they all blurred into one another the more I looked at them.

"Could I get one of these?" I asked my protectors quietly so I wouldn't draw the attention of the artist.

"You need magic in you in order for this particular charm to work," Tristan answered. "You could get one, but it won't have any magical effect on you." He clenched his jaw. I could tell my binding wasn't only hurting me. I nodded and we kept walking.

I saw beautiful necklaces and bracelets that were infused with different enchantments. It was all so breathtaking.

A group of children sat around a man wearing a sparkling top hat, black suit and a cane that intermittently changed between a staff and a flute. He would dance with the cane, then play the flute while casting spells that shot sparks around him. The children giggled and applauded.

Cotton candy magically appeared hovering in front of the visitors, tempting them to buy some by placing the money in the floating dish next to it. Some witches had their faces painted like cats; the whiskers popping to life and twitching. Some had butterflies painted on, the wings flapping and shimmering around their faces. I looked at everything around me in wonder, my mouth dropping open.

"What does the Bloomston festival celebrate?" I asked.

"Jerome Bloomston," Tristan answered. "He wrote the first doctrine which led to the creation of the council of Elders."

"Kind of like the constitution?"

"Sort of, yeah."

"Oh, so that's why the Elders are playing hookie to be here," I said.

"Yup," Lexi said "I wish there was a festival celebrating me." She wagged her eyebrows.

"Knowing you," Tristan said, "there probably will be."

Lexi chuckled.

"Can we go on some rides?" I asked, looking around at the fun around us. I was all but jumping up and down, but I was strongly considering doing just that. I felt like a kid again and I was having a hard time containing my excitement. Tristan grabbed my arm and pulled me behind one of the shops. Lexi rushed after us.

"Selena, please. I know you are excited, but you have to control your aura. It is blinding." Tristan was staring into my eyes, almost pleading with me to understand the importance of this.

"Okay, I'm sorry. I didn't know. How do I contain it?" I asked, not breaking eye contact. His green eyes were sparkling, and I almost couldn't breathe.

"Try to just keep it reeled in. Imagine that you are sucking the light from around you, into you. Get it?"

I nodded. Lexi had her back to us, watching as people walked by, making sure we weren't noticed. I took a breath and closed my eyes. I imagined what Tristan told me to and I heard him let out a breath.

"Thank you."

I opened my eyes to see him still staring intently at me.

"So it worked?" I asked astonished. He nodded and let go of my arm.

"I hope I didn't hurt you. I just wanted to get you out of sight before anyone noticed."

I shook my head. "I'm fine."

We walked back onto the street and immersed ourselves in the crowd.

"So… can we go on the rides?" I gave Lexi and Tristan my biggest puppy dog look while still making sure to keep my aura reeled in. They both laughed at me.

"Fine," Tristan said reluctantly, but he was smiling, so that was a good thing.

"Alexis? What are you doing here?" A small, blonde woman walked toward us hand-in-hand with a lean, light-haired man. I recognized them immediately.

"Oh, wow! Hey, Mom. Hey, Dad." Lexi said as they came closer. "We're just… checking out the fair."

"How nice. Oh, Selena, look at you! It's been so long!" Lexi's mom gave me a fierce hug, her large brown eyes sparkled.

"Hi, Angela. What brings you here?" I asked, releasing her hold. Mark, Lexi's dad, shook my hand formally. His ash blond hair so light, the graying at his temples almost blended in.

"We moved back here last year," Angela said.

"Lexi told me you guys were moving out of town; I didn't know she meant this. Then again I just found out about this place so…" I laughed.

"We knew you were well taken care of, between Alexis and Tristan, so we thought it would be nice to come back home. How are you adjusting to things, dear?"

"As good as can be expected I guess. It's a lot to take in but it's all very fascinating." I smiled politely.

"Well you make sure to let us know if we can help you settle in." She patted my hand, then turned to hug Tristan. "Tristan, how've you been?"

"Good, Selena's been keeping me busy," he joked.

"I'm sure she has," Angela laughed. "We'll let you guys enjoy the fair. Maybe you can stop by for a visit while you're in the city," she offered.

"That would be nice," I said.

"Yes, but I don't think we'll have time. If anything changes we'll let you know," Tristan said.

Angela nodded, "I hope I see you all again soon." Angela hugged us all again, and Mark nodded curtly.

"That was a nice surprise," I said.

"Yeah, it's great seeing them," Lexi said. "I was tempted to stay with them instead of the hotel, but I wanted to leave them out of all this."

We went to the Ferris wheel first, since I was still working up the nerve to try that rocket ride. The line was blessedly short, and within a few minutes it was our turn.

"You know what? I think I will sit this one out, you know, keep an eye on things," Lexi said moving her way out of the line. Tristan's mouth fell open for a moment before it ended up in a tight line. I heard Lexi laughing as she made her exit. I couldn't help but smile myself.

The frail old man in charge of the ride looked us over once before saying, "Two dollars."

"Dollars? I thought you would have magical currency or something," I joked.

"They take every currency here, since we all come from different places around the world," Tristan explained.

I reached into my pocket for some money, but before I could get any out, Tristan had paid the man and was giving me a weird look.

"What?" I asked.

"You're like a man. You want to carry the bags and pay for rides. Do I even want to know what kind of relationships you've been in that made you this way?"

I was a little stunned.

"Shouldn't you know? You watched me all the time, right?" I snapped.

"I tried to avoid those moments – Lexi was there for those days." Tristan clenched his jaw.

"Well, then, no, you don't want to know about the douche bags I went out with." I was quiet a moment, "And, I don't know. You're my protector," I said using air quotes, "I didn't know there were rules for this kind of thing. It's not the same as a date." Though the idea of Tristan being my date was exciting.

"Just let me take care of you." He cleared his throat and shook his head. "I mean, let me take care of the details, okay?"

"Fine," I huffed.

We were seated on the ride, and I looked for the bar that strapped us in place.

"Uh…" I started frantically.

"What's wrong?" Tristan asked.

"Where's the bar?" I hissed.

The old man laughed, "Magic will keep you in place, no worries," he said as if I should know this already.

I gulped. This was almost as scary as being shot up in the air. I looked to Tristan for reassurance.

"Relax." He smiled. "The magic restraint also acts like a shield and will protect you if the ride were to malfunction. Much better than just the bar humans use."

"Malfunction?" I felt like I would fall out of the seat, until I felt a slight pressure on my lap, relieving my stress. Tristan chuckled.

The seat was smaller than I thought it would be, and the right side of my body was firmly pressed against Tristan. I tried to give him some room by shifting, but I had nowhere to go. The ride jerked up one notch and the next riders were seated. Once the ride was full, it started its smooth circulation.

The view was amazing when we reached the top; I could see the treetops that covered the plush grass, the hills rolling like waves. Just behind them the silvery reflective surfaces of the corporate buildings shone, splattering the nearby foliage with rainbow specks as the sunlight bounced off the glass. Birds scattered from the trees, speckling the sky. I could see everything for miles.

"This view is gorgeous," I said aloud, leaning forward as if that would give me a closer look.

"Yeah, it is pretty nice. I forget how beautiful this place can be." Tristan gently pushed me back into the seat.

"Are you sure I'm not keeping you away from all this?"

Tristan ran his hand through his hair.

"Selena, I don't understand why you can't grasp how important you are. This is just a place, and I can visit whenever I want. I haven't lived here for fifteen years, and I'm surviving. Believe me, it's not that big of a deal. Why does this bother you so much?"

"I don't know. I guess, especially now that I don't have any powers, I feel like I'm not worth it." I tried to keep my tone light, so it wouldn't sound like I was having a pity party. "You and Lexi have your own lives to lead, and I have done nothing to prove to you or myself that I am the one the prophecy is about."

Tristan turned and took my face in one of his hands. I think I stopped breathing for a second. His hand was warm against my skin, and I had a sudden urge to close my eyes and savor the moment.

"Listen to me. This is the last time I will say this: You have abilities I have never seen any one person have. Even when you couldn't control it, your powers were great. You fit the description, you had your awakening on the same date the prophecy said, and your aura is the most beautiful thing I have ever witnessed. When you're happy, you light up. No one else has that the way you do. Now stop feeling sorry for yourself and questioning your gift."

He released my face and looked back out at the scenery. I couldn't stop staring at him. I never expected him to say those things. I tried not to read into it too much. He was here to protect and guide me, and that's what he was doing.

"Alright, I won't bother you with that again." I looked down at my hands, and I played with my mother's ring. "Thank you," I added, "for everything you do." Tristan stiffened slightly and kept his eyes averted.

"No problem."

"So, how…?" I wanted to find out more about Tristan but I didn't want to pry.

"How what?" He asked facing me again.

"How do you have your own house? I mean you don't have time for a job, do you? Lexi mentioned a trust, but I wasn't sure how that worked. Do you get an allowance or is it a lump sum up front?"

Tristan chuckled, "Bit of both, but mainly my family was well off, so I was always taken care of."

I noticed he had used the past tense for his family.

"Where are they now?" I asked as kindly as I could. Tristan closed himself off; he shook his head but stayed silent. He had mentioned his mother once, how she had taken him to the Aracali ruins, but that was all I had gotten from him so far.

The ride came to an end, and we went to meet Lexi, who was waiting for us at the exit.

"Did you two have fun?" She asked in a sing-song tone. Tristan's jaw clenched.

"Yeah, it was fun," I answered, making Tristan's expression relax a little.

All three of us went on a few more rides after that, but I couldn't bring myself to try the crazy one.

"I think we should try to find an Elder," I suggested. "I mean we had fun, saw trinkets, and I'm tempted to buy some by the way. So unless you want me to spend money, I strongly suggest we do something more productive."

"We can try, but I wouldn't get my hopes up," Tristan responded. "These Elders have a serious egotistical complex. They won't want to help."

"I think we should try anyways," Lexi encouraged. So we walked around in search of my only possible salvation.

"What am I looking for exactly?" I asked after a few minutes of people watching.

"Anyone who looks old, like retired old," Lexi explained.

"Okay, so if you're old you're automatically an Elder? Shouldn't there be some kind of requirement met?"

"There are requirements actually," Tristan started. "Once you hit 70, if there is an opening, you are eligible to join the Elders, but you have to pass a series of tests firsts. Like knowledge of spells, ethics, control of powers, stuff like that. It's easier to just look for someone old because the only old people at the festivals that aren't working are either Elders, or going to look for the Elders," he finished, never moving his attention away from the crowd in front of us.

"Okay then." I started looking. There really weren't any older people around at all. There were many teenagers wearing colorful clothes with sparkles on their face. Kids ran around playing with different toys and sparking magic at whim. I understood then, watching this crowd, how they could be themselves here. If any human ever saw this in their neighborhood, there would be problems. It was nice that in the face of worry and threat, witches still found a way to enjoy themselves.

I saw a young girl dancing around her mother, carrying a plastic wand with tinsel draping off the tip. She waved her wand and giggled at something in the distance. I followed her line of vision and saw that she had levitated a table with trinkets for sale on it. The woman working in the kiosk tried to push the table down absently as if this were an everyday occurrence. It probably was. The mother scolded her daughter and the table fell gently back in place. I smiled at the sight, and again felt the loss of my powers. I also realized how much I missed my mother.

That thought sharpened my focus. I needed to find an Elder, and now. Suddenly I was annoyed that I had wasted any time on rides and shopping. I should have been searching the entire time instead.

We kept our eyes open, constantly searching. The afternoon wore on and I was starting to lose hope. I found a bench and dropped my weight onto it. Lexi and Tristan stood next to me, knowing there was nothing to say at that moment. My gaze scoured the crowd, I saw a group of girls laughing and teasing each other, a bald head walk by, a child on the shoulders of his father—wait. I looked back at the bald head. I followed it with my eyes and saw that it was rimmed with white hair around the back of the head and ears.

"There!" I pointed. Tristan and Lexi looked where I was pointing and nodded. Then they were on the move. Again I found myself struggling to keep up. Their speed was unmatchable by humans. I frowned at the word.

"This will not end well," I heard Tristan say ahead of me. I was jogging to keep up to their walking pace.

"Excuse me?" Lexi said once we were within ear shot of the man. He turned his cool blue eyes towards us.

"Yes?" He answered, his voice a little hesitant.

"We were wondering if you knew of any Elders here?" She asked.

"I was just heading over to them myself actually. I suppose it would be alright if you came along." He started walking then, and we followed politely behind.

"Thank you," Lexi said. A moment later the man walked into a tented area, and as we crossed the threshold, I saw a group of older men and women talking together at the back end. There were a few people in seats in front of them, and one of the seated women raised her hand.

"You may speak," one member of the older group said.

"I was wondering if you would be able to perform a spell to heal my son. He's very ill and I haven't been able to find a witch with healing abilities."

"What is your offering?" An older man asked.

"I apologize that I don't have much, but whatever you seek I will give you."

The group converged and discussed the matter in a silent conversation. It was the weirdest thing I had ever seen. They were standing in a circle, looking at each other, but no one's lips moved. Finally one lady nodded her head.

"What abilities does your son have? And what is his age?"

"16 and telekinesis, telepathy, and shield spheres so far."

"Bring him to us tomorrow at noon."

"Oh, thank you! Thank you so much!" The woman openly wept, wiping away her tears on her shirt sleeve.

"We will use him around the courts as payment."

The woman nodded reluctantly. I wasn't sure why. It would be better to have a son working in the courts than dead.

She stood up and rushed out as if afraid they would change their minds.

"What is this?" I whispered to Tristan.

"It's odd actually. This is the kind of meeting they would grant in court. Not at a festival. They must have had a lot of people track them down today. I don't think that will make them in a better mood for our request."

"Well we're here, they're here. We should at least try, right?"

Tristan looked at me, and studied my face for one brief moment before nodding his head.

"Right." He raised his hand.

"Young man, you may speak," one of the female Elders said.

"I was wondering if it wouldn't be too much of an imposition to request a private meeting. My issue is rather personal," Tristan spoke as politely as possible, always maintaining eye contact. The Elders looked at one another for a moment.

"Alright, my name is Victoria, you may speak with me in private," the woman answered. My heart raced with excitement. This could be it! Maybe she could undo my binding right here and now. I was so excited until I saw Victoria look at me strangely. Tristan turned to see what she was staring at, and his face fell slightly when he saw me. I cursed myself under my breath and reeled in my aura. Damn it, it was probably too late.

"What is your issue, boy?" Victoria asked. Her white streaked, black hair was up to her jaw and framed her face. Her skin showed her age, wrinkles around her eyes and mouth were indications. She was a short, petite woman, only reaching Tristan's chest.

"It pertains to the prophecy."

"Ah, I thought that might be it," she said, eyeing me suspiciously.

"We need complete discretion please. We do not want anyone knowing she is here, nor the issue to which I am about to speak," Tristan said. He sounded so weird, like he was talking from another time. Lexi stood behind me, with one hand on my shoulder for support. Victoria nodded in agreement.

"There has been a binding spell placed on her, and I am quite certain it was unauthorized."

Victoria's brown eyes bulged slightly, and her lips became a thin line.

"That is impossible," she whispered.

"All due respect, but it's not."

Victoria started to walk toward me but thought better of it. She looked around and motioned for us to follow her.

We left the main tent and she led us to a deserted area between other tents behind it. As we stopped she circled me. She raised her arm and placed her hand above my head and travelled it around my shoulders and body.

"Damn. How is this possible?"

I was shocked at her language, she seemed too proper to curse.

"We believe Darien was able to obtain the ritual information and conduct the spell."

"You know only an--" she stopped short.

"Yes, only an Elder has the ability to perform it, but I did not want to be so bold as to imply any Elder's involvement. Is there any way to break it prior to expiration?" Tristan asked with urgency in his voice.

"There may be, but I do not have all the details. You will need to see someone else for that." She looked at me with a hint of sadness in her eyes.

"Would you be so kind as to give us a name?"

Victoria thought for a moment. She was probably weighing our dire need for the name against her need to keep the Elder's information private.

"Jeremiah Lacour. But you didn't get that from me, understood?" She ordered, her eyes hardening. Tristan nodded.

"Is he here now?"

"I'm afraid not. You can see him tomorrow at 10:00 am sharp. There will be an appointment set up for you. Again, I had nothing to do with it." I was glad Victoria could override that uptight clerk. Next Friday my ass.

"Thank you very much for your help. Just one more question if I may?"

Victoria nodded.

"Can you tell when the spell will expire?"

She let out a sigh at that, and looked away. After a moment she nodded, and swallowed hard.

"Upon her death."

10. HOPELESS

The walk back to the hotel was a blur. I couldn't think of anything except my permanent binding. If we couldn't find a way to break this stupid spell, I would be human for the rest of my life. I didn't even have the hope of waiting for the spell to run its course.

Once we were inside our room, I took my shoes and jeans off and sprawled on the bed. I didn't care that I was only in my underwear with Tristan there. I didn't care what Lexi was trying to say. I just wanted to be left to my thoughts. I rolled over onto my side, curled my legs up and rested my head on my arm.

I heard Tristan and Lexi arguing in the bathroom. I wasn't sure what it was about and I didn't care. I wished they would keep this one a silent conversation, so I could get some peace and quiet. I heard some shuffling and Lexi saying, "Just go." Tristan sighed, and then it was quiet for a few minutes. I didn't want Tristan to leave. I wasn't in the mood to talk to anyone, but it was comforting to know they were there.

I felt the bed beside me sink with body weight. Lexi was probably in her comforting mode now. I saw the shadow of one hand hover over my hair for a second before dropping down to the bed. I saw the hand lift again, and it softly caressed my arm. I relaxed a little and rolled over to hug Lexi and probably cry on her shoulder. Only when I turned, it wasn't Lexi I saw.

Tristan lay beside me, curled on his side facing me. His hand stopped mid-air when I rolled over. He was staring at me with uncertainty in his eyes. My heart swelled, and I couldn't stop the tears that were coming. I moved myself closer to Tristan and curled myself into his chest. He ran his fingers through my hair, and the feeling was wonderful. It was such a shame it was tainted by this terrible turn of events. I grabbed the front of his shirt in an attempt to get closer and I cried. It wasn't the ugly cry thankfully, just the 'my heart actually hurts' cry.

"I promise you. I will do everything in my power to break this spell," he whispered in my hair. I nodded, and the tears soon stopped. We stayed like that for a long time, until eventually, I fell asleep.

When I woke, I was on my stomach, and my arm was across Tristan's chest. It took me a moment to get my bearings. I looked up and saw that he was lying on his back awake.

"How long have I been sleeping?" I asked, trying to focus.

"About four hours," he answered.

"And you stayed with me the whole time?" I couldn't believe it.

"I wasn't sure when you would wake up and I didn't want you to be alone."

Oh man, he really wasn't making it easier for me to stop having feelings for him.

"Where's Lexi?"

Tristan's jaw clenched. "She went to get some food. It's almost dinner time."

"Oh." I relished in the feel of his body next to mine, my arm across his muscular chest, and then I remembered the morning's events.

"When you were talking to Victoria, you spoke differently. Was that out of respect?"

"Yes, and it always helps to speak as others did in that time."

"That time? How old was she?"

"Oh, probably around 130. I was estimating the time frame when I spoke to her, but I must have been close."

"130? What? She looked like 80 tops!"

"We age differently. Our aging process slows when we hit 30 or so. We live much longer lives than humans."

"How much longer?"

"Well it varies of course, but on average we live to be 170 to 200 years old."

"Ew! Oh God. So if my powers stay bound forever will I die like a human or live a long but miserably magic free life?"

Tristan let out a sigh.

"You would live a miserably magic free life, unless you got hit by a bus or something."

"Oh great, something to look forward to." I realized he hadn't specified how long that life may be.

"Let's just wait and see what happens," he said.

"Do you think this Jeremiah guy will be able to help?"

"I hope so. Victoria seems to think so, he must know enough about bindings to give us something to work with. Just try to stay positive. We will know more tomorrow."

I moved my arm. "If you want to get up, I understand," I told him, hoping he would stay. He seemed to think about it for a minute before answering.

"I think you could use another five minutes," he said, clenching his jaw again. I hid my smile and rested my head on his chest. I heard him take a quick breath and hoped I wasn't crossing any lines.

"Thank you," I whispered.

"You've been thanking me a lot lately. You don't have to."

We stayed like that for a few minutes when the lock rattled on the door. Tristan instinctively moved, and I lifted my head to let him. He looked down at me and gave me a quick smile as he got up. Lexi had the bedroom door open in one hand and a bag of food in the other. The smell woke my senses.

"Hey! You're up. Are you doing okay?" She asked as she set the food down on one of the tables. I nodded and looked at Tristan.

"I had great support. Thank-" I stopped myself. "It was appreciated."

Tristan looked up at the ceiling. "It's the same thing," he said under his breath. "Stop thanking me."

I smiled, but ignored Tristan. "What's for dinner?" I asked Lexi instead.

"Orange chicken, pork fried rice, teriyaki beef, you know, the best of Chinese food." My stomach growled.

We ate quietly, and when we finished I started clearing the table when the bags and cartons vanished.

"Oh!" I exclaimed, taking in the clean area before me.

"Yeah, hotels do that," Lexi smiled. "Perfect house-keeping."

"Very cool," I said sitting back down. "Thanks, Lex. That hit the spot."

"I knew it would!" She chirped, throwing a look at Tristan. I smiled and went to take a shower. I let the water run for a few minutes before getting in. The hot water beat down on my head and back and melted away my tension. I took my time washing and conditioning my hair. I scrubbed myself down, trying to get all the negativity off me, and by the time I was done, I actually felt a lot better.

After about a half hour I got out and wrapped a towel around my body, and then started towel drying my hair. I realized too late that I didn't bring a change of clothes to the bathroom with me. Oh well, Tristan just saw me in my underwear, so who cared?

I made sure my towel was secured and went out into the bedroom.

"Aw, look who's getting all comfortable," Lexi teased.

"Shut up. I forgot to grab my clothes." I walked to the closet and grabbed my comfy clothes. I caught Tristan looking at me from the corner of his eye, and then he cleared his throat and shifted uncomfortably. I went and dressed in the bathroom, putting on my usual shorts and tank. I grabbed a brush and came out to the room again. "Sorry. I hope I didn't make you uncomfortable," I told Tristan as I brushed through my hair.

"Uh." He shrugged, and shook his head. "I've seen you in less. It doesn't bother me."

I smiled and continued brushing my hair. I braided it and let it fall heavily down my back. I got in bed, and although I just woke up from my very long nap, I was still tired. My lack of sleep the night before definitely had something to do with that. I really loved my sleep. I sat up, leaning my back against the pillows, and I felt a sense of something missing. I realized a moment later that it was Tristan. How is it that I already missed the feel of him next to me?

I contemplated asking to sleep next to him, but I didn't want to come across as needy. Or freak him out. It was a surprise that he let me get as close to him as I did at all, and I knew not to push my luck. But still, I was tempted. I shifted my thoughts to something more bearable.

"Hey is there any way I can learn to see my aura?" I had been thinking about it all morning and wondering what everyone else saw.

"Well, you could learn, the same way humans teach themselves these things, but you won't be able to see it to the extent we can," Lexi explained. "You'll see just a haze of color. That is an option though, just until you get your powers back... well your full powers. Because once you do, you will have no problem seeing other peoples' auras." Lexi jumped on the bed next to me.

"How do you manage to sound so sure that I will get my powers back?"

"Because I have faith that everything will work out."

"Alright, how do humans teach themselves to see auras?" I asked.

Lexi shifted and sat cross-legged facing me.

"Your aura is basically a magical field of energy that you can train yourself to become sensitive to," Lexi started. "Start by trying to see the aura around your hands. Once you get used to that, you can try to see it around your head the way we can."

"Okay…" I looked down at my hands. Tristan sat on the edge of his bed watching us.

"Alright, get comfortable and relax," Lexi said. I followed her instructions, taking a deep breath and collecting myself. "Stretch out your right arm, with the back of your hand facing you."

I did this, and studied the back of my hand.

"Now spread your fingers, and try looking at the area in between them, but let your eyes become a little unfocused."

Again, I did this, allowing my vision to relax, creating a blurry image of my hand.

"You should start to see a golden outline around your fingers, and the more you study it, there's a chance it can change colors."

Staring at the back of my hand, I concentrated on trying to see this glow. I sat there for a few silent moments, with Lexi and Tristan watching me. Suddenly, between my fingers, I saw a light shimmering. I gasped as it came into better focus.

"I think I see it," I said in awe. Though it wasn't anything impressive. "It's not that bright."

"It's only because you don't have full access to your powers to see it the way we can," Tristan said.

"That's still pretty neat," I said, but I was a little discouraged, worried that I would never get my powers to see what they could. My focal point suddenly changed as my mother's ring caught my attention. I felt the familiar pull into the sapphire stone, the illusion that it was moving and drawing me into its depths. I found myself in the familiar white room, where my mother had once shown me why I shouldn't feel guilt about killing those bad witches. I felt the presence of my mother again, and knew she was trying to tell me something. I focused on sensing her and could tell I was close.

"Pretty cool, huh?" Lexi said, breaking my concentration.

I blinked rapidly, and looked at my mother's ring again, hoping I could know what she was trying to tell me, know how she would try to comfort me this time, but I couldn't get back.

"Yeah," I whispered, disappointment in my tone.

"Don't worry, you'll see it the way we do," Lexi said, misinterpreting my behavior.

"Sure, sure," I said, and smiled to show I was fine with it. "Thanks."

"Anytime." Lexi beamed. "The more you practice that, the easier it will be to see it around your head."

"Okay," I said, still distracted. I flattened my pillow and moved my body down so that I could lay my head on it. Tristan reached over and turned the bedside lamp off, submerging the room in darkness. It took only a minute for my eyes to adjust enough to see Tristan lying on his back on the other bed. I turned myself on my side so that I could face him, and watch him sleep like I had the night before.

I had barely finished adjusting my position when Tristan rolled onto his side and faced me. We stared at each other for a few long moments, neither of us breaking eye contact. Once it became too much to bear, I looked away.

"Goodnight, Tristan," I whispered, and looked back into his eyes.

"Goodnight," he said still facing me.

"Goodnight!" Lexi yelled. I started laughing, and Lexi and Tristan joined in.

"Hello, beautiful," a male voice said. I found myself in a yard that looked an awful lot like Tristan's. I knew I was dreaming, but it felt too real. I turned to see who had spoken and saw Darien standing behind me. His short brown hair was combed neatly, his sunglasses sat on the bridge of his nose, obscuring his brown eyes. The black t-shirt he wore showed off muscular arms I didn't know he had, and light blue jeans hung off his hips. He smiled lazily at me as if this meeting were perfectly ordinary.

"What do you want, Darien?" I asked, crossing my arms over my chest.

"I missed you," he said, "and how you looked in that dress." He tilted his head as if to get a better view. I realized then that I was wearing the tight red dress that I had worn to one of our dates.

"Why are you here? Did you get bored of mentally tormenting me?" I asked, trying to keep my uneasiness in check. Darien strode toward me.

"No, that never gets old." He smiled. "I sincerely wanted to see you."

"I'm sure." I rolled my eyes. Darien shrugged.

"Believe what you want."

"Why did you do it?" I asked after a silent moment.

"Which part?" Darien asked, almost boasting.

"Why did you bind my powers?" I swallowed a sob.

"Because I had to," he answered as if this were perfectly obvious. "I couldn't have you running around thawrting my plans. I mean, after you killed all those witches I sent for you, I knew you had to be stopped."

"Well you won... I'm human now. Are you happy?" I snapped.

"Not really, I was enjoying watching your powers develop… well until they got in my way." Darien paused in thought for a moment. "What if I proposed a solution?"

"What kind of solution?" I asked hesitantly.

"What if I told you I could unbind your powers for a small price?"

"I'd tell you to go to Hell," I whispered.

"So bold, considering you don't know how much worse this binding will become." Darien circled me. "Aren't you at least curious to know what my terms are?"

"No, I don't want to owe you anything."

"All I was going to suggest was you help me perform one tiny ritual in exchange for your powers."

"Oh, is that all?" I asked sarcastically, but wished I had my powers to control the elements and throw Darien away from me. I narrowed my eyes. "I wouldn't help you kill a fly."

"That's too bad," Darien said, taking off his sunglasses. He looked me in the eye and ran the handle of his glasses down my arm. "We could work wonderfully together."

"Go crawl into a hole and die, Darien." I jerked my arm away, but Darien came closer. He ran his fingers along my jaw, and I turned my head out of his reach.

"Such a shame," Darien shook his head, but didn't move away from me. "You had a lot of potential. I'd hate to see you die."

My heart raced at his words. Was he going to kill me now? Could he kill me in a dream? "You don't scare me," I said, proud that my voice didn't deceive me.

Darien chuckled, "Sure I do." He grabbed my face roughly and kissed me hard and fast, before I woke up panting. I crept out of bed and went to the living room so I could move freely. I didn't want to wake the others. I paced back and forth thinking about my dream. Was that real? Did I really just talk to Darien or was that all a figment of my imagination? I thought it through and replayed the conversation and realized Darien had to have been there. Should I have been so quick to dismiss his offer? If he could get my powers back, wouldn't it be worth performing a small ritual? No, not if it was a ritual that could hurt others, which, with Darien, it probably was. This was so frustrating.

"Selena." I turned to see Tristan walk into the living room. He sat on the couch beside me. "Why are you up?" he asked.

"Bad dream. I'm sorry I woke you."

"Don't be, I couldn't sleep well either. What was your dream about?" I contemplated telling Tristan what it was and decided it wouldn't hurt to talk it out with someone. I sat heavily on the couch and placed my head in my hands. I let out a yelp as the couch suddenly shivered and shook beneath me, pulling its sides in around me. Looking down, I saw that I was now sitting in an arm chair.

"What just happened?" I asked.

Tristan smiled. "The furniture automatically adjusts to hold however many people are using it. Look." He approached the couch, ready to sit, and it expanded, adding another seat for him.

"That is actually pretty crazy," I said in awe.

"You'll get used to it." He leaned back. "So, tell me about your dream."

I told him about Darien and his proposal, leaving out the kiss at the end. Tristan sat silently for a few moments while he processed this.

"I'm glad you refused to help him," he started. "Though I can't help being curious as to which ritual he would want your help with."

"I know, I feel the same way, but I can't take the chance of owing him anything."

"I agree. Hopefully Jeremiah will be able to help us so you won't need Darien or his schemes."

"Hopefully," I whispered. "He said the binding would get much worse. What does he mean?" Tristan looked away. I felt the urge to cry from my fear and frustration. Tristan moved closer to me and pulled me into his arms, but he didn't say anything, and that scared me. I knew he had information he wasn't sharing with me, but my fear of discovering what it was outweighed my curiosity.

I looked up at Tristan and he was looking at me, warring with some emotion I couldn't decipher.

"Selena," he whispered as he lowered his face to mine. Then he closed his eyes tightly and moved away. "You should try to get some sleep. We don't know what we will have to deal with tomorrow." He wrenched himself away from me and headed back to the room.

"Tristan," I called after him and he paused, back still turned to me. "Can you please forget your stupid rules for one minute?"

He turned, studied me for a heartbeat before taking two long strides and pulling me up to stand in front of him. He cupped my face and kissed me, engulfing me with his torn emotions. I felt the rawness of his desire and the power of his resistance. Our lips moved together like we had been kissing our entire lives. I wrapped my arms around his neck, pressing our bodies closer together. Tristan ran his hand up my arm and through my hair, clenching it at the nape of my neck before he pulled away, breathing heavily. He looked at the floor and then met my eyes.

"I'm sorry," he whispered.

"I'm not," I retorted, my frustration evident.

"You are undoing me," he said, hand still clenched in my hair. "Can't you see how dangerous this could be?"

"No," I whispered. I really couldn't.

Tristan clenched his jaw, pressing his forehead to mine. We stood like that for a moment before Tristan fully released me.

"We need boundaries," he said as he left the room and left me reeling.

11. I WAS NEVER ANY GOOD WITH POETRY

The next morning I woke to the sun streaming through the window. Tristan and Lexi were surprisingly still asleep. I had no idea what time it was. I quietly got out of bed and went to the bathroom to wash up and get dressed. When I came out, Lexi and Tristan were still sleeping. I checked the time on my cell and saw that it was only 6:30 am. I had time to kill.

I walked to the large window, wanting to see the beautiful view this time of day. I pulled the drapes open a little bit and saw that the ledge of the window was wide enough to sit on. I sat on the ledge and turned my body so that my feet were up on it too, and my back was against the wall framing the window. I leaned my head on the cool glass and admired the various types of trees, watching the sun finish its rise over them, bringing them to life. It looked like a black and white movie turning into color right before my eyes.

As I sat there, I thought about meeting Jeremiah and hopefully breaking the binding spell. I thought about Tristan, and how it felt to be in his arms the night before. I thought about the Hidden City, and everything it held secret. I lost track of time.

I heard some movement and knew someone was awake.

"Lexi," Tristan called, and I knew he was trying to wake her up. "Lexi, where is Selena?" There was an urgency in his voice that I had never heard. Almost panic.

"I'm right here," I answered, looking around the curtains. Tristan was standing above Lexi, one arm on her shoulder no doubt shaking her awake. Lexi had sat up and was looking around for me. I saw relief flood their features.

"What are you doing over there?" Tristan asked, walking toward me.

"I was up early and figured I might as well enjoy the view."

Tristan stood facing the window, looking out at the vast expanse of greenery.

"It's not like you to wake up early, and you're already dressed." He took in my short jean skirt and white tee. "Come on, Lexi, we need to get ready too. Selena actually beat us to something," he joked walking toward the closet.

"Oh, ha-ha." My voice dripped with sarcasm. "You just wait. If I ever get my powers back, you'll wish you could keep up with me."

Tristan raised an eyebrow. "Oh really? You're awfully sure of yourself, considering you haven't been able to beat me in a fight yet."

"Well I didn't have full use of my powers. That doesn't count."

Tristan laughed and went to the bathroom. I was surprised at his upbeat mood considering our exchange last night. He seemed fine, like nothing happened. I, on the other hand, was a mess of emotions.

Ten minutes later he came out wearing only a towel around his waist. I groaned internally. I envied the water beading on his chest, and dripping down the wet strands of his hair. What a beautiful creature. He looked at me then.

"What? I forgot to get my clothes," he said, mocking me. "I'm sorry. I hope this doesn't make you uncomfortable."

"You're an ass. And no, it doesn't. I've seen better," I lied.

"Good to know," he said, grabbing his clothes and heading back to the bathroom.

"And what happened to boundaries!" I yelled after him. He stuck his head out of the bathroom door.

"Right," he said clenching his jaw. "Sorry." He closed the door.

"What boundaries?" Lexi asked.

"Just something Tristan wants," I answered looking down. Lexi shook her head and rolled her eyes.

"Hey Romeo, can you hurry your ass up, please? I need to get ready too," Lexi yelled through the bathroom door a few moments later.

Tristan came out wearing jeans and a black button-down shirt with the sleeves rolled up to his elbow. It really wasn't fair; he never looked bad. Ever. His face was tense and I could tell he closed himself off again. I almost wished I hadn't reminded him of the boundaries; I didn't want him to get cold again, but it was torture seeing him like that, like putting a treat on a dog's nose and telling him not to eat it.

Tristan and I sat in silence while waiting for Lexi to get ready. I looked at the clock and saw that it was almost 9:30. We had to leave soon.

"Look, I really am sorry," Tristan said breaking the silence. "I was just joking around, but you're right. We need to remember to keep boundaries, or even jokes could lead to… other things." He smiled.

"Hey, they're your rules, not mine. I'm just trying to follow them."

Tristan nodded. "It's for a good reason."

"If you say so," I mumbled under my breath.

Lexi came out then, dressed in a pale green summer dress. Her usually spiky hair was combed down flat, making her look like Tinker Bell.

"You guys ready?" She asked.

"You're joking right? We've been waiting for you," I said, trying to repress my laughter.

"It was just habit to ask I guess. I just- oh shut up, Selena." She walked toward the door. "Let's go." Tristan and I followed her out. It was time to meet Jeremiah Lacour.

As we walked toward the court a thought came to mind.

"Is there any way that I could see the prophecy? I mean, everyone keeps telling me what the prophecy says, but where is it?"

"No one knows where the original is," Tristan answered. "It was written by a psychic who received the information, but we believe someone stole it so no one would ever find out about you. Not for your protection, but for the removal of hope for our people."

"So how do you guys know what it says?" I asked confused.

"It was donated to the library before it was stolen, and some of the witches who had a chance to read it paraphrased it. We don't know if there was more information that was lost as it was passed down."

"Who predicted it?"

"That's a mystery too. Apparently his or her name was recorded, but since whoever it was never came forward, it was never made public. Maybe they were afraid they would get hurt for spreading the prophecy. We don't know."

"You guys are putting a lot of faith into something you don't know much about."

"Selena, you really need to get some more of that in you," Lexi added.

"More of what?" I asked.

"Faith. Just believe that there is something great out there that will take care of you to make sure the prophecy gets fulfilled," she said smiling.

"I do... well I believe there is something greater than us, I'm just having a hard time with the rest of it." I thought for a few moments. "So where is the paraphrased version?" I asked.

Tristan's jaw clenched again. "It was stolen from the library a few months ago. Before your birthday as it turns out."

"I thought the library has a spell on their books to make them automatically return once they've been checked out," Lexi commented.

I was getting confused.

"Yeah well, apparently whoever took it was able to remove the spell on it and take it out of the library without checking it out," Tristan explained.

"Or it was the ritual," Lexi said.

Tristan opened his mouth to respond, but I cut him off.

"Why would a prophecy be in a library? Shouldn't it be framed in a museum somewhere, with lasers protecting it or something?" I asked.

Tristan smiled and shook his head. "Although prophecies are extremely rare, they are kept in the library for the public. It's the law that everyone has access to any and all prophecies. However, the library did keep the original document encased in a frame. There were replicas that could be checked out. The library is very well protected and the prophecy should have been safe there, which makes these disappearances mysterious."

"Replicas? I didn't know you guys had a photocopying machine," I teased.

Lexi spoke up, "We don't use photocopiers; we have magic, remember?"

"Which was our downfall apparently," Tristan added. When he saw my curious expression, he continued with a sigh. "We use spells to replicate documents, and in the case of the prophecy, they too were kept in the library. If anyone checked one out, it would be recorded as if the original itself was checked out. Someone broke that spell too though. Once the original document was taken, all the replica's disappeared with it. Same thing happened with the paraphrased version." Tristan's jaw worked in frustration.

"That's the version most people remember anyway," Lexi started, speaking animatedly. "What really happened was that there was a ritual performed on the night of the summer solstice in 1988... or was it 1989? I'm not sure, but anyway, this ritual was responsible for destroying the prophecy. Not only that, but it made everyone who read it forget the details. That's why some witches doubt it ever existed, or that there is a savior, or more importantly that they need saving. No one knew who would do such a thing or why." Lexi's voice lowered into a whisper. "Some speculated it was to protect the one mentioned in the prophecy, you." She winked at me. "Other's thought it was to deter your fulfillment of it. The main theory was that people were harassing whoever foresaw the prophecy to come forward and claim the vision. So the psychic performed the ritual to protect him or herself and their family."

"How do you know that's what really happened?" I asked.

"My grandfather used to tell me stories when he was alive. He had so many conspiracy theories that most people thought he was crazy and dismissed his tales. I treasured every one. Apparently there was a huge investigation after the original went missing, but the Charge couldn't find the psychic or the prophecy. Eventually some people's memories came back but only bits and pieces which is how the paraphrased version came to be. But most people forgot that a ritual was performed and think the prophecy is just missing." Lexi smiled triumphantly.

"Jeez," I said. Wanting to see the prophecy I understood how removing access to it could deter me from my purpose. I could have used the reassurance reading the prophecy would have provided.

We arrived at court then, and silence fell upon us. We walked in quietly, only breaking the silence when we reached the counter.

"Yes?" An older man asked, obviously not as into customer service as his colleague yesterday.

"We have an appointment with Jeremiah Lacour," Tristan answered.

The man looked down into his books.

"Name?" He asked. Crap, Victoria hadn't taken our names, how would she know who to make the appointment for?

"Selena Arturro," Tristan whispered. The man raised his eyebrows, appraised us and nodded.

"You may proceed to room 125. It'll be down that hall and on your left." He motioned to a long corridor to our right.

"How did she know my name?" I asked when we were no longer in earshot of any clerks.

"You're well known," Lexi whispered. "They may not know what you look like, but everyone knows who you are." Great.

We found the room easily, and Lexi knocked on the door.

"Enter," I heard a muffled voice from the other side of the door. I took a deep breath, and Lexi turned the knob. We walked into the room and I was surprised at its simplicity. It was a standard square room with a floor-to-ceiling window instead of one wall. There was a dark wood desk in the center with a chair behind it and two chairs in front. It was so plain compared to the beautiful lobby.

The gentleman standing, looking out the window was tall and lean. He turned and greeted us with a smile. His black hair was graying at the temples and he had piercing blue eyes with minimal wrinkles around them.

"Elder Lacour?" Tristan asked, standing straight, already changing into his polite mode.

"Yes, how can I help you?" He asked kindly.

"We requested to see you today, because we know you are somewhat of an expert on spell binding."

"You do, do you? And how do you know this?"

"Your reputation precedes you, sir."

This earned a smile from Jeremiah. "Alright, what do you need from me exactly?"

"Well sir, we have discovered that someone has placed an unauthorized binding spell on the one mentioned in the prophecy."

Jeremiah's eyes hardened, but made no other reaction to the news.

"So you must be Tristan then. And Alexis," Jeremiah said, looking at Lexi. His eyes traveled over me, "And you must be Selena. Interesting."

"Yes sir," Tristan responded. Though I knew he wished he wouldn't have been recognized.

"What makes you think she's bound?" He asked.

"I don't think, sir. I know for a fact. What we need to know is if there is any way to break the binding prior to its expiration."

"I see." Jeremiah approached me and looked me over. He moved his hand over me quickly. "I'm sorry, Selena. Your powers do appear to be bound after all."

I wanted to say duh, but resisted the urge.

"Please, Elder Lacour, can you help us?" Lexi pleaded. He licked his lips and thought for a moment.

"What I am about to tell you is not to be repeated. I must place a spell to prevent you all from telling anyone the antidote to breaking a binding. You will be physically unable to speak the words to give this information out."

My heart skipped. Oh my good God, there was a way to break it! I made sure my aura was behaving. We all nodded in unison.

Tristan held out his hand, and Jeremiah clasped it. He looked to Lexi who placed her hand on top, and then they all turned to look at me. I stepped forward and placed my hand over Lexi's.

"By the power within, I swear not to repeat what I am about to be told."

"I swear," Lexi and Tristan said in unison.

"I swear," I followed course.

We all let go and stepped back.

"Breaking a binding can be quite simple, so long as you have everything you need. For starters, you will need an Elder to perform the ritual, but I suppose I can step in that role for you."

We all let out a collective sigh of relief. We were expecting it to be difficult to find an Elder to tell us how to break the spell, never mind perform the actual ritual.

"The next item you will need, you must figure out on your own. I can only tell you this:

Below the living is the dead,

Though it is small, it's also said

That size alone does not matter

This item, with power, will not tatter

In the darkness it is found

Though it grows within the ground

In the place where death does dwell

But under the name that goes with bell and bell"

Jeremiah finished speaking, and we all looked at each other. What the hell? I saw Lexi typing in her phone and hoped she was making a note of that clue, because there was no way I would remember it all.

"Bring that item to me, and I will perform the ritual for you." Jeremiah walked over and opened the door. Tristan nodded, and we walked out, slightly puzzled.

We didn't say a word until we were outside again. In the sunlight, the dreary riddle seemed almost comical.

"Do you guys have any idea what he's talking about?" I asked. Lexi shook her head.

"No," Tristan said, "but I think we should get some food, go back to the room and brainstorm." So we did just that. We grabbed some sandwiches from a deli, which I thought would be a normal walk-to-the-counter-and-place-your-order type of deal, but no. As soon as we entered the quaint deli, paper sandwich bags appeared in each of our hands. The bags had a list of ingredients and bread options. Tristan and Lexi didn't hesitate as they selected what they wanted by pointing to the ingredients with their fingers. As soon as they were done, the bag inflated, their sandwich materializing instantly. Creeped me out. It took me a minute to feel comfortable enough to place my order. Sandwiches in hand, we sat down on the patio for a few minutes to enjoy our meal. I wished we could have stayed there longer, it was a beautiful place to be, but I knew we would have to discuss the clue in private.

We reached the hotel room, and I sat on the sofa. I jumped up as it began its transformation into an arm chair.

"I don't like that thing," I said, giving the sofa a wide berth.

"Oh," Lexi said, taking out her phone. "It'll settle in a minute. Just come and sit down." She sat in the seat and immediately it shifted and extended, adding another cushion.

"Should stay steady now." Lexi smiled and I tentatively sat down.

"That is seriously weird," I said in awe.

"Yup," Lexi wiggled her eyebrows, focused her attention back on her phone and started scribbling on the hotel stationary. As soon as she finished writing, she waved her hand over the sheet and threw it against the wall. The sheet shimmered and the writing transferred onto the white wall like a projector.

"I always feel that it's easier to figure things out when you're looking at it," she explained.

"Selena, your aura is glowing again. What are you thinking?" Tristan asked, sitting in the armchair. It stayed an armchair.

I smiled. "Is it wrong for me to get excited about this? I mean is it too premature to get my hopes up? I could get my powers back!"

I looked from Tristan to Lexi who were both smiling, but still reigning in their own hopes.

"It's okay to be hopeful, but don't get ahead of yourself," Lexi said. "Unless we can figure this riddle out, nothing is going to happen. Let's just focus on this first, okay?" She rubbed my shoulder.

"Okay, fair enough." I looked at the words on the wall and thought about the meanings.

"Let's try it one line at a time," Tristan suggested. "Below the living is the dead… like Hell?"

I shook my head, "It would have to be somewhere we can go."

"I'll tell you a story sometime," Tristan commented.

"What? You've been to Hell?" My mouth gaped.

"No, not exactly. But there is a veil between the living and the dead where damned spirits are. I saw Hell through it."

"But you haven't been there yourself, right?"

"No, I guess not technically."

"It's not a bad idea," Lexi started, "but I agree with Selena. I think it would be somewhere more accessible."

"Okay, what about a cemetery?" Tristan offered.

"Yeah, that seems to make sense, and we know it's something small. Maybe it's buried in the ground?" I commented.

"Yes, small but full of power. It sounds like this thing is indestructible." Lexi added.

"'In the darkness it is found,' that could be going back to maybe being buried somewhere?" I asked.

Lexi was taking notes on all of our ideas. "Could be," she said.

"What about, 'Though it grows in the ground'?" Tristan asked. We were all silent, thinking it over.

"A… plant maybe?" I suggested. Lexi wrote it down.

"'In a place where death does dwell' that could be referring back to a cemetery… right?" Tristan asked.

"Why would there be two clues for the same thing?" Lexi asked, looking up from her paper.

"Just write it down," he almost snapped. Lexi did.

"I have no idea what the last line means." I said, reading the words over and over again.

"I'm not sure either," Tristan said. Lexi shook her head as well.

"Are there any cemeteries around here?" I asked.

"Yes, there are quite a few actually. Many witches like to be buried here because of the magical elements in the earth," Tristan explained.

"Alright, let's start with the locations."

"I'll be right back." Lexi stood and walked out the door.

"Argh," I yelled as the couch began to adjust itself. "Stop it." Immediately the shimmering stopped. "Oh, I get it now. It listens." I laughed.

Tristan smiled. "I told you, you'll get used to it."

"So, where's Lexi going?" I asked, looking at the door through which she just left.

"Not sure, but I'm sure she'll be back soon."

"I've been curious about something." I looked over at Tristan who was sitting casually in the arm chair.

"What's up?"

"I wondered what it would be like to have a silent conversation. I have received things from Darien, but I haven't really been able to do what you and Lexi do. If I get my powers back and can use telepathy, will you have a conversation with me?"

Tristan smiled, and it made his whole face light up.

I would be honored to. Tristan said in my head. It was kind of nice to have someone that I actually wanted in there for once. I sent a mental thank you, and Tristan's eyebrows pulled together.

"Did you just say 'thank you'?" He asked.

"Yeah. You could hear that? We can have a conversation then?" I asked excitedly. Tristan sat up straight.

"It's weird; usually I can only have a conversation with someone who is telepathic too. Otherwise I can send things to them, but I can't hear their side. I wonder how I can hear you. I mean it's not as strong as if you were telepathic, but I can definitely hear it."

"So, you can read my mind?" I cringed. I really hoped not. I suddenly felt the urge to put up a mental wall. It would be terrible if he knew all the things I thought about him.

"I don't think so. Think of a number, but keep it to yourself like a normal thought. Don't send it to me okay?"

I thought I understood what he meant.

"A number from one to ten or…?" I asked. Tristan laughed.

"If I could read your mind, it could be anything and I would know."

I nodded my head and thought of what number I wanted. I decided on 5678. Not the most original, but it didn't really matter. I kept it in my mind only.

"Okay I got one," I said. Tristan sat silently for a moment, just staring at me.

"I got nothing. It's blank," he finally answered. I let out a sigh of relief.

"Okay, how about now?" I mentally sent the number to him as if I were saying it out loud. His lip twitched into a half smile.

"5678?"

"Yes! That's amazing! How is that possible?" I asked.

"I have no idea. When Lexi gets back I'll ask her if she can hear you too. Maybe it's just because your power is inherently strong, so maybe that aspect lingered? I don't know for sure though."

I don't either. I sent mentally.

Tristan laughed out loud, but silently he said, *You're getting good at that.*

"This is so cool! Is there a limit to how far we can be and still hear each other?" I said out loud.

"With normal telepathy, no. It comes in really handy sometimes, let me tell you. But with you, I'm not sure if the same rules apply."

Lexi came back in then carrying a folded pamphlet in her hand.

"Okay, I just went to get a map so we can find the exact locations of the cemeteries here. Assuming it's in the Hidden City at all." She moved the vase of flowers onto the floor, unfolded the paper and laid it flat on the coffee table. I ignored her for the moment, more consumed by the telepathy.

"Lexi, you've got to hear this," Tristan said excitedly. Lexi looked up from the map. "I can hear Selena telepathically. We can have a conversation."

Lexi's expression was one of confusion.

"How?" She asked.

"We don't know!" I blurted. "All I know is that when I sent him something directly he could hear it, but if I had it as just a normal thought he couldn't."

"But she sounds different. Like it's not as clear as you, but it still comes through," Tristan added. "Can you try and see if you can hear her too? I wonder if some remnant of her magic is making telepathy available to her."

"Sure!" Lexi looked at me and sent a sentence. *Hey Selena, how's it going?*

Really, you couldn't send something more creative than that? I sent back. Tristan chuckled, and Lexi looked at him quizzically.

"You didn't hear that?" Tristan asked surprised.

"Hear what?" She retorted. Tristan and I looked at each other.

"You heard what we both said?" I asked Tristan.

"Yes, but that's only because you two weren't blocking the conversation. You were sending it out freely so anyone with the ability could hear it," he explained.

"I can't hear Selena," Lexi said with a hint of disappointment in her voice. Then dawning crossed her face. "But that means you have some kind of connection with her, Tristan. Have you been able to hear her for a while?"

"No. Not that I know of anyway, this is the first time we tried."

"I'm pretty sure you would have noticed if you could before. If Selena even thinks your name during a thought you could probably hear it," Lexi analyzed.

"How would you know that?" I asked.

"I've seen it before. I told you we discover different powers all the time. Tristan has developed an affinity for you. He can connect to you on a different level mentally. You may have just opened your connection right now, just by trying to talk telepathically." Lexi laughed, "Just make sure when you get your own telepathic powers that you block your thoughts from others when you have these kinds of conversations, or, like you saw, everyone will hear. Right now though, only Tristan can hear you, so you're good."

"How do I block it?"

"Before you send anything, just picture a cord between you and the person you're talking to and only think of them when you're talking. It's not that hard really, and the more you do it the easier it gets."

"So, I don't have any powers, Tristan does?"

"Pretty much. Congrats, dude," she added looking at Tristan.

This could be very dangerous. If I thought of Tristan he would be alerted to it. I would seriously have to control my thoughts. Add that on top of trying to keep my aura in check and my brain will be in constant overdrive. Still it was nice to have this kind of connection with Tristan.

"Yeah, like I said, it could come in handy," Tristan said.

"That was random," Lexi said.

"How so? I was just agreeing with Selena," Tristan said, looking at me for back up.

"Oh God. I didn't say anything, I was just thinking it."

"Oh. Sorry," he said. "Sounded stronger that time… I could have sworn you actually said it." Tristan's eyebrows knitted in confusion.

"You guys will figure it out. Can we focus on this now please?" Lexi asked, slightly irritated.

"Aw, you're mad you can't hear Selena too, aren't you?" Tristan teased.

"It does suck slightly, yes," she answered.

Tristan chuckled. Lexi gave him the evil eye and the arm chair he was sitting on moved from under him causing him to fall on the floor. Anger flickered in Tristan's eyes for a split second and the pen Lexi was holding flew out of her hand and hit her right in the forehead. I started laughing. That was the funniest thing I had ever seen.

Lexi's face flushed with anger, but she kept it in check, calming down after a moment.

"We need to work on this now. Try to be mature," she scolded.

Tristan raised his eyebrow. "You want me to be mature? You started it!"

"Right, and that's a very mature thing to say too."

"Will you guys cut it out? Lexi's right, we need all the information we can get," I said, looking at Tristan, but I was trying to repress my laughter. He let out a sigh.

"Alright, what have we got?" He knelt on the floor beside the map to get a closer look. Well that and he probably didn't want to get the chair. Lexi had her pen in hand again and she was reading the map carefully.

"There are seven cemeteries in the Hidden City." She proceeded to circle the location of each one. "This one here," she pointed to one of the circles, "is the closest one. We could start there if you want."

"This could take forever!" I said. "We don't know what we're looking for, and we're going to have to dig in random places. What if we don't find this thing? What if we never figure out the riddle? What if we get caught?" I asked, starting to panic. "I don't want to go to magic… jail or whatever. Or, what if, like Lexi said, it isn't even in a cemetery in the Hidden City? The world is massive! We may never find it, and I will be stuck like this!"

"Whoa, calm down," Tristan started, "I know it's like trying to find a streaker in a nude beach, but we have to try and stay positive and keep a clear head. We'll figure this out."

I smiled at his analogy, took a deep breath and calmed my thoughts. I couldn't let myself lose control or I would definitely never figure this out.

"And as for getting in trouble," Lexi chimed in, "We will be very careful, use practical spells, and remember that the risk we take will be worth it to get your powers back." She wiggled her eyebrows.

I shook my head, but said, "Okay, let's start there tonight and see what happens."

Lexi tapped my shoulder, "We're going to need some shovels."

12. DIG, DIG, DIG.

We waited until dark to start our search. We weren't sure how much digging we would be doing, so we needed to make sure we weren't seen. The cemetery was too far to walk to, so we rented a car. We were all piled up into a nice, discreet, Volkswagen Jetta. The rental store had a wide variety of cars though, from all eras and countries, and even had their own carriage sedans. Those were cool; they were spherical carriages but with car tires and ran without horses. Of course, the cars in the Hidden City didn't actually have engines. Like the carriages, they were spelled to run, and at any speed, but without emitting any noxious toxins into the clean city air. Tristan insisted on driving, Lexi was the navigator with her map, so she sat up front, and I sat in the back feeling useless.

We had purchased the items we needed that afternoon. I had bought black, tight, skinny jeans and calf-high boots since I hadn't packed anything appropriate for grave digging. Tristan bought some flashlights, and Lexi picked up the shovels. Since she was the smallest and least threatening, no one would be suspicious. Could you imagine if Tristan went to buy three shovels? I laughed at the thought.

"I'm not that intimidating," Tristan said out of nowhere, looking at me in the rear view mirror.

"Damn it, Tristan, get out of my head!"

"Hey, you're the one who needs to control your thoughts."

"Whatever. And yes, you are intimidating. All 6 feet of muscle. You're an ape." I huffed and crossed my arms over my chest. This was going to be annoying.

"I'm 6'2" for the record, and I have a neck. Lexi would tell you I don't look like an ape. I'm lean," he announced.

Lexi laughed, "I agree that you're more lean than bulk. As for manners: definitely an ape."

"What is this? Pick on Tristan night?"

Lexi and I laughed.

"Alright, alright, you're not an ape," I amended.

"I already knew that, but thank you so much for confirming," Tristan said sarcastically, and chuckled.

"You're going to make a left at the next street," Lexi instructed. Tristan nodded and changed into the left lane.

"Why are the traffic laws American. What if witches come here from England or something?" I inquired.

"It's just driving," Tristan answered. "It's like when you go on vacation, you adapt to the place. They made this American because the majority of people know those laws."

"Explain to me again why we're driving instead of teleporting," Lexi said.

"It looks less conspicuous than popping up out of nowhere at a cemetery. Normal is good sometimes." Tristan smiled.

"Yeah, right," I mumbled

"Besides, I like driving. It clears my head," Tristan added.

I looked out my window at the night blurring past. The full moon would help illuminate the grave yard. My stomach lurched in anticipation. We still weren't entirely sure how to approach this task. All we could agree on was that we would go to the cemetery and see what we found.

Lexi was going to use a detection spell, though she told me that it wasn't going to be accurate, since we didn't know exactly what we were looking for. We would try to locate anything that had power infused into it, and once she found something, we would dig it up. It wasn't the best idea, but it was all we had for now.

"Okay, park over here," Lexi ordered. "We'll walk the rest of the way." Tristan pulled up to the curb, and we quietly got out of the car. It was a clear, warm night, and the moonlight was comforting. We walked a short way but had to cut through the woods to get to the cemetery.

Tristan was in the lead as always, and Lexi brought up the rear. I tried to keep up with Tristan's long strides, and Lexi was trying not to step on me. I really hated that I was so slow compared to them. I pushed myself to go faster which wasn't a good idea. I tripped on a fallen branch, cursed and put my arms out instinctively so I wouldn't land on my face.

Tristan turned in time to see my descent, and with one quick motion, wrapped his arm around my stomach, turned me and tucked me into him so his body was pressed against my back, steadying me. I stood up straight, and Tristan let go.

"Thanks."

"Be careful, will you? There's only so much we can do to keep you safe, without you hurting yourself, okay?"

"Okay, sorry. But you move like the Flash. I can't keep up." I pouted.

"Alright, I'll slow down. I forget sometimes. We're almost there anyway." He was right. Before I knew it, I could see tombstones ahead. I resisted the urge to run in. I'm not sure why, but I always found cemeteries fascinating. As I got closer I saw rows and rows of headstones, statues, crosses, and tombs in a clearing. I suddenly felt overwhelmed again.

"Where do we even start?" My eyes were taking everything in at once. And let me tell you, there was a lot to take in. This place was huge.

"I will feel the place out for any enchanted objects," Lexi said. "You guys keep your eyes open for any clarification of the riddle." She walked closer to the graves, shovel in hand. I looked at Tristan.

"There are seven cemeteries? Are they all this big?" I asked.

"I'm not sure. This is one of the more populated cemeteries, I know that, but I don't know how big the others are." He walked towards Lexi and started looking around. I had no idea what I was doing there. I didn't have any powers to cast spells. I had no idea what to even look for, all I could do was dig if it came to that.

"Selena, come here," Lexi instructed. She and Tristan stood on a patch of ground clear of headstones or markers.

I raised my eyebrows as I approached them. "What's up?"

"Hold still for a minute," Tristan said. He raised his arms and moved them around us, a light fog appeared, and as he continued, it grew thicker until it settled on the ground and around us. He then brought his hands down to his chest and brought them together as if they were holding an invisible basketball. He pressed his hands on Lexi's shoulders, then mine, and then his own.

"We don't want to attract any attention to ourselves, so this will keep people from seeing us at all," Lexi explained after seeing my confused expression.

The fog made the cemetery downright creepy. I felt like I was in a horror movie, hiding from an abnormally large man with a mask and knife.

Not long after we started our search, Lexi called out, "Guys, we have a problem."

Panic rose within me as I rushed toward her, Tristan reached her before I did.

"What's wrong?" Tristan asked, searching the area.

"Sorry, I probably shouldn't have sounded so dire," Lexi said. "It's just that there are dozens of graves that have enchanted objects buried within."

"We can't dig up that many," I said, sounding defeated.

"It's ok," Tristan said. "We just need to apply the clues of the riddle." He paused, looking around the cemetery. "Like headstones for a woman named Belle, or something to do with plants or flowers, like Laurel, or any other plant."

"Sounds like a plan," Lexi said. I just nodded.

We walked around for a long time, just looking for any items relating to the riddle. Lexi was spell casting, still trying to find any magical objects.

It was an hour later when Lexi called us. Tristan and I jogged over to see what she had found.

"I think I found one, John Birch," she said. "I'm not sure exactly what it is, but there is definitely something in this grave." Tristan nodded and started shoveling. I joined in a moment later, pressing the point of my shovel into the soft grass. I couldn't get it in far enough, so I had to step on the head to push it into the ground. By the time I got my first shovelful, Tristan had gotten five. I sighed and kept trying.

"This is going to take a while," Tristan said. "Hang on a sec. I want to try something." I stopped shoveling and took a step back.

Tristan held his hands over the grave, palms down. The ground started shaking, the dirt crumbling apart in the process. Tristan lifted his hands and the dirt shot up into the air.

And fell on us.

"What the hell, Tristan?" Lexi yelled, shaking dirt from her hair. I started laughing.

"Sorry, I didn't realize my own power, I guess. I will tone it down next time," Tristan said chuckling.

"That was awesome!" I chirped, earning a modest smile from Tristan. He reached over and dusted off my hair and shoulders.

"I guess we didn't need shovels after all. You may have mentioned that before we spent the money," Lexi said.

"I wasn't sure I could do that. I just figured I'd try." Tristan dusted the dirt off his own head and arms. "Besides it's better to be over prepared."

I looked at the ground and saw a perfectly rectangular-shaped hole, and the coffin it contained. The brown wood that I could tell had once been shiny, was now dull and worn in areas.

"Go ahead Tristan." Lexi obviously didn't want to get anywhere near any bodies.

"I think it would make more sense for someone smaller to go in," he said. "It would be easier for me to help one of you out of the hole afterwards."

"You're 6'2". The grave is what, normally 6'. You can get yourself out," Lexi countered. I rolled my eyes and jumped in the grave.

"Selena!" Tristan yelled. "What are you doing?"

I looked up at them. "Well, you two are obviously chicken hawks, and we can't waste any time arguing over stupid things. Plus, I've been feeling useless, so at least I can help this way."

Tristan shook his head.

"I'm not scared at all actually," Tristan said. "I just thought it would make sense if the 'big ape' as you say it, isn't the one needing a hand out of a grave." He glared at Lexi.

"Whatever. Why don't you just make the ground lift you with your powers?" Lexi retorted sarcastically.

"Ha. You're just jealous that I'm such a badass, and you're not," Tristan teased.

"You got the ass part right." Lexi crossed her arms over her chest.

"Guys, just shut up!" I yelled.

They did.

I squeezed to the side of the coffin and braced myself. This lid had a latch on the side, so I flipped it open and gripped the edge. I mentally counted to three and lifted the lid.

And I gagged.

I know in movies they say the smell of a decomposing body is the worst thing, but it's one thing to hear and a completely other thing to experience it firsthand. The body was pretty much unidentifiable. The skin was missing in chunks, revealing parts of bone as bugs crawled over the face and hands. Strands of hair remained on the skull, a partial skeletal grin spread across half the face, one eye completely gone. The only way I was able to tell the sex was by the suit on the body. I shivered at the sight. I held my breath and started searching for any small objects.

"Ugh!" I yelled. "This one is still fresh."

"Yeah, been dead a few months," Lexi said reading the headstone.

"Would the object be in such a recently dug grave?" I asked.

"It's hard to know for sure," Tristan said. "Sometimes enchanted objects appear and reappear as needed."

I looked back at the corpse, "This guy was definitely not embalmed." I swallowed hard.

"We don't embalm the bodies here," Tristan said.

"We must give to receive, remember?" Lexi added. "We believe our bodies are meant to feed the earth after we die. Even the coffin dissipates and provides nutrients. Now, hurry up."

"Okay, I see a ring. It's a simple silver band and also a pendant necklace. It's got a thin silver chain, and the pendant itself is a blue stone. There's nothing plant-like," I reported. Lexi stood two feet from the edge. She peered over, but never stepped any closer.

"Can you toss them up?" She asked.

"That's just mean!" I yelled up. "That would mean I would have to touch the thing."

"I'm sorry, but the only way to tell if they're infused is to touch the object itself," Lexi said.

"Are you kidding me? Why aren't you down here then?"

Lexi shot me an innocent look. "I was trying to get Tristan to go, and you just jumped in."

I rolled my eyes.

"That's pretty messed up," Tristan said. Lexi just shrugged, all eyes and innocence.

I sighed and regretted it. The smell permeated my senses, making the bile rise again. I swallowed it down and leaned into the casket. I reached for the hand first and then pulled back.

"I don't think I can do this."

"Yes you can," Tristan said. "You are strong. Just try not to think about what you're actually doing."

I clenched my fists, and looked up at the velvet black sky. Okay, I can do this, I can do this. I chanted silently. I unclenched my fists and looked at the ring rather than the hand it was on. I reached out and touched the ring only. The silver band wrapped loosely around the decomposing finger. I pulled it gently, and it came off easily. I let out a sigh of relief that I didn't have to touch the body itself.

"Okay, I got the ring. Here." I threw it up and Tristan grabbed it.

"No magic in this one. Try the necklace," Lexi said after a moment.

"Damn it," I whispered.

Tristan tossed the ring back down to me and I put it back on the finger. There was no way I could get the necklace off without touching the body. I swallowed hard, still trying to keep my nose closed off to the odor. My hands shook as I reached for the necklace. It was clasped at the back of the neck of course, so I had to wrap my arms around the head. Bugs scurried out of the way, and I jerked my hands back. I shook my arms in case any crawlers found their way on them and took a deep breath. I looked back into the casket.

My stomach lurched. Okay toughen up, Selena, you don't want Tristan thinking you're a wimp. I wanted to un-think the words immediately. I knew Tristan would have heard that. I looked up and saw he was staring down at me, eyes glistening, and his mouth a tight line. Ugh.

I had an idea then. The chain was a decent length, so I grabbed it where it was on the chest of the body and lifted it up with the tips of my index and thumb. I barely touched the rotting skin.

Once I had it lifted an inch or so, I pulled the chain around gently until the clasp was at my fingers. My heart rate accelerated as I tried not to touch the corpse. I kept imagining that it would come to life and grab my hand or something. I undid the clasp, and slipped the necklace off with great relief.

The ground shook, making the dirt walls loosen and cave in around me. I tried to move, but my feet had somehow sunk into the ground.

"Selena, come on!" Tristan yelled to me.

"I can't move!"

Lexi ran over to the side of the grave I was on and knelt at the edge, reaching her arm out.

"Can you reach my hand?" She asked panicked.

I tried and stretched but we were a few inches short. Tristan jumped in and climbed over the casket to me. He grabbed my legs, trying to pull them up from the ground. The walls were still caving in, the dirt falling with such force it closed the casket lid, and was up to my thighs. Tristan was still prying my feet out of their soiled trap.

After a few seconds, his frustration skyrocketed and he used his powers to force the dirt away from me. He lifted me easily, placing his arm under my knees and throwing my arm over his shoulder. He cradled me like that and stood on top of the coffin that was now completely covered in dirt. With the height of the coffin, and the constantly falling dirt, he was able to clear the edge of the hole and place me flat on the ground. He hoisted himself up after, and grabbed me to move away from the edge. We stood and watched the grave fill itself back with dirt.

"Oh my God, Selena, are you alright?" Lexi cried, rushing over to me.

"Yeah, I think so." I looked at Tristan standing next to me. He was looking down at me with a mixed look of relief and panic.

I looked down into my hand and saw that I still had the necklace. I handed it to Lexi, whose eyes narrowed as she touched it.

"This is what I sensed." She held it for a moment to determine its abilities. "It's infused with a protection spell… ironically for this exact purpose; to protect the remains and allow the wearer to rest in peace. If anyone disturbs the grave, it awakens a quicksand spell." She was quiet a moment, sensing the necklace's attributes. "It's why the ground caved in, and it renders itself worthless," she finished.

"Worthless? How?" I asked. Just then the sparkling blue stone changed, becoming foggy, and darker, and finally settling its transformation to a dense, black stone. The chain tarnished, giving the necklace a cheap, costume jewelry look.

"Damn, can't even get any money for our troubles," I joked. No one laughed. I looked at the grave and saw that the ground looked completely disturbed. People would know we were here.

"Is there any way to fix that?" I asked Tristan, pointing to the sunken in grave.

"I can," Lexi said smugly. "I can reverse the effects of a spell, remember?" She merely looked at the site and it became completely and flawlessly undisturbed. Except for the few shovels full Tristan had taken initially. Tristan waved over the rest of the area filling in the dirt he had removed. It was as if we were never there.

"That's still awesome," I said, missing my powers.

"I know, right?" Lexi chirped, shooting Tristan a dirty look. I took a step and gasped in pain. Something must have happened to my ankle during all that mayhem.

"Come sit down," Tristan said, noticing my limp. I sat at the step of one of the tombs.

"So what do we do now? I don't know how many more graves I can rob," I said, resting my foot.

Tristan knelt in front of me and started untying my boot laces.

"What are you doing?" I asked.

"I just want to make sure you're not seriously hurt."

"I'm fine," I protested.

"Just let him check, will you?" Lexi chimed in. Tristan continued loosening the laces. "As for what we do now," Lexi continued, "We have to continue what we've been doing so far. Eventually we'll find something."

"No way," I said. "This will take forever. I can't wait that long; I feel myself withering away." I admitted. Tristan looked up at me sadly for a moment before returning to my boot, finally taking it off as gently as he could manage. It hurt like hell anyway, and I took in a breath through clenched teeth as a reaction.

"I'm sorry," he said when the boot was finally off. He took my sock off and studied my ankle. Even from where I sat I could see it was swollen. "Can you move your toes?" He asked. Lexi stood behind him studying my ankle too. I wiggled my toes, and it caused a sharp pain in my ankle that made me cringe.

"Okay, good. It's not broken, just sprained," he diagnosed. "We should probably leave, and come back another night."

"No!" I shouted. "I don't want this taking any longer than it has to. I will just sit here and you guys do whatever you need to do. I wasn't helping that much anyway."

"How can you say that?" Lexi asked. "You were all up in that dead guy's coffin."

"That's nothing. But that's not the point. The point is, let's stick with the plan, okay? I will stay right here."

Tristan and Lexi exchanged a glance.

"Okay. Let's finish this," Tristan said.

They returned to the search.

I really wished I had my powers. I would have been able to heal myself in two seconds and cast detection spells with Lexi, feeling more helpful. I shook my head to clear the longing, and watched Tristan and Lexi roam the cemetery.

As the night progressed, I started to get sleepy. Not having the adrenaline of work keeping me awake, I leaned my head back against the tomb door and closed my eyes.

"Selena, wake up," Tristan whispered. I opened my eyes to see him standing above me, "It's time to go."

Lexi stood beside him; she carried the three shovels in one hand and my boot in the other. I stood up, making sure not to put any weight on my bad ankle, and Tristan came to my side, allowing me to lean on him for support. We slowly waddled through the woods for a minute before Tristan let out a huff of impatience. He picked me up, and continued his usual, quick pace. I wrapped my arms tighter around his neck, enjoying the ride.

"Did you guys find it?" I asked, trying not to get my hopes up.

"No. Hopefully it will be in the next one," Tristan answered.

We reached the car all too soon, and Tristan put me in the back seat. I lay down and decided to continue my nap. I fell asleep almost instantly and woke again when we reached the hotel. Lexi unlocked the door, while Tristan helped me inside.

"Dibs on the shower!" Lexi called, running to the bathroom before anyone could protest. I hobbled past a mirror on the wall and gasped.

"What is it? Your ankle?" Tristan asked concerned.

"No, my head. What the frack?" My hair was like a tangled nest, dirt was caked in it, and I couldn't even run my fingers through it. Soil and muck was smeared on my face, arms and chest. I looked like I had been the one dug up. What a mess. I picked at my hair, and gave up quickly.

"It's all part of the job," Tristan responded. I looked at him and gave him a dirty look. Then I felt better because his hair was all messed up too, and although he wasn't as dirty as I was, he did have a smear here and there. He sat on the window ledge waiting for Lexi to finish.

I sat on the bed and took off my other boot and sock. I realized then that it was a bad idea getting skinny jeans. Looking at it, my ankle was already so swollen it pushed against the material. I contemplated how to get around this. I could ask Lexi for help, but let's face it, if I wanted anyone to help me take off my pants it would be Tristan. Then again, Tristan had his boundaries thing. I decided to just try it on my own.

I stood and started hopping to the living room.

"Where are you going?" Tristan stood up and walked toward me.

"I need to… just go to the living room for a minute. You can stay here."

"Helping you take off your jeans isn't a boundaries issue… I don't think," he said contemplating the situation.

Ah, hell. "This is ridiculous. And embarrassing. You need to stay out of my head."

"And you need to block your thoughts."

"That's not fair! Anytime I think your name you hear everything that goes with it!"

He nodded in defeat. "You're right. But let me help you."

I hesitated a moment and then sat back on the bed and tried to keep my mind blank. He tentatively pulled at the cuff of my pants around my ankle, and I jerked my leg back in pain.

"This is going to suck, isn't it?" I asked. He looked up at me, and then back to my foot.

"Pull your pants down so I have more room to pull it over your foot," he instructed. Again, I tried so hard to keep my mind blank because there were way too many responses I could have thought up for that.

I unbuttoned my jeans and pulled them down to my knees. Tristan pulled them off my good foot so that he could focus just on my bad one. He tugged again gently, and again I jerked back. "This isn't going to work," he said standing up. "Do you have any scissors?" He asked.

"No. Maybe Lexi has some in her bag of tricks."

Tristan went and knocked on the bathroom door.

"What?" Lexi called out.

"Do you have any scissors?" Tristan asked. It was silent a moment.

"Actually, no. Sorry," she answered.

"Damn," he said under his breath. He knelt in front of me again. "Okay, I have an idea." He pulled the cuff of my jeans up as high as they could go – which wasn't very high, these jeans were sealed on. He somehow managed to get them about three inches above my ankle. He grabbed the edge of the fabric in his hands and pulled. His arms flexed, making his veins very visible, and the material made a ripping sound. I looked away from his arms and back to my jeans and saw that he had torn the cuff of my jeans apart.

"Holy crap," I said under my breath. Tristan pulled my pants back down and over my foot easily. "Thanks."

"And you were going to try and do that alone," he teased. I shrugged my shoulders.

Lexi came out already dressed in her sleep wear, and stopped short, taking in the view. I was sitting on the edge of the bed in my black tank top and underwear, Tristan was kneeling on the floor in front of me holding my jeans. Her eyebrows rose.

"Oh, wipe that look off your face," I said. "Tristan was just helping me take off my jeans because they were too tight around my swollen ankle."

"Uh huh," she said getting into bed.

Tristan stood up and went to shower next.

"You guys are so weird," Lexi said when she heard the shower running.

"What do you mean?"

"You guys say you have boundaries and crap, but you are so into each other. I don't get it."

"There's nothing to get. His job is to protect me, and I," I thought about my role in this platonic relationship. "I have to let him."

"So stupid," she mumbled and rolled over onto her side. "You know what?" She lifted her head and faced me, "You're not allowed to sleep in this bed tonight. I don't care where you go, but it better not be here. If I wake up and find you here, you'll be sorry." She moved so she was in the middle of the bed and spread her arms and legs out, taking up all the space.

"Well it's 5:00 am, so it's no longer night. Your rule doesn't apply," I argued. She sat up.

"Listen to me very carefully. You are not allowed in this bed. Final." She fell back down and closed her eyes letting out a content sigh. I knew she wanted me to sleep beside Tristan, but I had no idea why she was pushing us so much. He didn't want that kind of relationship, and I had to respect that. She was just making this harder on me.

Tristan came out of the bathroom wearing a tank top and sweat pants, and he looked at Lexi quizzically.

"Why is she sleeping like that?" He asked.

"She kicked me out of the bed. She says I will be sorry if she finds out I slept beside her."

"Why? Did you guys get in a fight?"

"Nope. Just Lexi being Lexi." I grabbed my towel and clothes and limped toward the bathroom.

"I should call Genevieve," Tristan said before I reached my destination. "She will be able to heal your ankle."

I paused and looked down at my foot. The idea was tempting, but I didn't think it was urgent enough to wake Genevieve and have her rush over here.

"I will be fine tonight. It can wait until tomorrow."

"You sure?" Tristan asked concerned.

"Yeah," I answered and went to shower. It was the best shower I ever had. I was so filthy from all the dirt and grime, and it felt fantastic to see the brown water at my feet as evidence that I was getting clean. I scrubbed at my face and washed my hair three times until the water ran clear. The smell of shampoo was infinitely better than that of decay. I dried off and dressed quickly.

When I came out, Tristan was sitting on the edge of the bed, leaning his elbows on his knees, and he held something white in his hands. He sat up straight.

"Here, I got some stuff for you," he said, motioning for me to sit on the bed. I sat and he again knelt on the floor in front of me. Turns out the white thing he was holding was bandage for my ankle. He took my foot and wrapped it securely. I winced at the pain, but didn't jerk my foot away. When he finished, he stood up and went to the living room. He came back with two crutches.

"When did you get this stuff?" I asked surprised.

"You take really long showers. And this place has pretty much everything." He smiled.

"Thank you. You saved me tonight and you got all this stuff, and I feel bad that I can't do anything for you."

"You can. Stop thanking me, that's all I want."

I shook my head. "Weirdo," I mumbled. Tristan chuckled.

"Um... did you get any ice by any chance?" I asked, feeling bad that I was asking him for something else.

Tristan cursed, "I knew I was forgetting something. Here let me try this." He held the crutches in one hand, bent down again and held my ankle with the other. A moment later a cooling sensation permeated my skin, instantly soothing it.

"How did you do that?" I asked.

"I can control air, so I just made it cold around your ankle."

"Cool," I said in awe. I looked over at my Lexi-conquered bed and sighed. I stood up and took the crutches from Tristan. They were already adjusted to my height and

I tried them out. I got the hang of it pretty quickly, and started moving toward the living room.

"Where are you going now?" He asked. I grabbed a pillow and blanket from the closet, and held them awkwardly, still trying to keep a grip on my crutches.

"The couch." I hobbled my way over to the black leather sofa to set up my bed, and it shifted, molding the cushions into a smooth, long surface and expanding the arm rest like a pillow. I chuckled at the sight. Tristan was right behind me.

"You can't sleep on the couch. Sleep on my bed, I'll sleep on the couch," he offered.

"This is hardly a couch now." I smiled. "Besides, how is that fair?"

"You're injured and you need a good night's rest."

"Look. It's the least I can do for you saving my life. It's no big deal really, and the other arm of the couch will be a good place to put my bum foot up on."

Tristan actually considered that for a moment.

"No. Come on, you're getting the bed."

I sighed, "You know, I know there are boundaries and blah, blah, blah, but it is a queen-sized bed. Can't we just share it? You can stay on top of the covers if it makes you feel better. That way no one has to get the couch."

Tristan ran a hand through his damp hair, his jaw clenched as always.

"Come on." He led me back to the bed, and pulled the covers back for me. I crawled in and it felt heavenly. It was so comfortable, and I was so tired. Tristan put a pillow under my foot and then laid on top of the covers on the other side of the bed. I was glad he wouldn't have to endure the couch. I fell asleep as soon as my head hit the pillow.

13. YOU REST WHEN YOU'RE DEAD

I woke up the next day and felt like... well, death. I was still so tired. I rolled over to get into a more comforttable position and fall back asleep when I saw Tristan wasn't beside me. I lifted my head and saw that Lexi was still asleep in the middle of the other bed. I got up, and the room swayed slightly. I almost felt drunk. I grabbed my crutches for support.

I looked in the bathroom, but it was empty, so I left the bedroom and went to the sitting area. There, on the couch, was Tristan fast asleep. Unbelievable. His blanket had fallen on the floor during the night, so I picked it up and covered him. He looked completely different when he was asleep. He looked so much at peace, it was relaxing just to watch him.

I went back to bed, still feeling exhausted.

I was lying on a park bench, enjoying the sun's hot rays caressing my skin. The trees surrounding me swayed gently to the soft breeze. The sun shone through the leaves, making them almost sparkle. I heard a noise and quickly sat up, swinging my legs forward. My eyes searched the area around me but I was alone. Only the paved path, surrounded by the clean cut grass, lay before me.

I heard another noise; a rustling like dried leaves underfoot. I stood and tentatively took a step forward. I distantly felt a pain in my ankle, but it was easy to ignore. I kept walking. Trying to determine the source of the noise, I crept forward to where the trees huddled closer together and blotted out the sun. Shadow engulfed me immediately, and I felt very cold.

The wind swept around me, ruffling my clothes and playing with my hair. I saw a figure dart behind the trees, and my heart rate picked up. I froze, not sure I wanted to follow.

Selena, over here, a voice said, and although my stomach dropped from fear, I felt compelled to obey. I walked forward and bumped into something solid, but there was nothing there. I pushed the air in front of me, and the invisible wall moved. The ground under my feet felt soft, plush even.

Come up here, the voice said.

"Where?" I asked, searching the dark forest ahead of me.

Follow my voice.

I did. I walked straight, until I hit another invisible barrier. I pushed it aside and as I kept walking I heard a loud slamming echo around me. The forest became darker, the ground under my feet cold and hard, my ankle protested in pain.

Up here.

I climbed higher and higher until my legs ached, and my breathing was labored. Sweat moistened my shirt as I kept the steady incline. It was so dark in this part of the forest, I couldn't tell where I was going, or what was around me. I hit another barrier, and I angrily pushed through it.

A welcome and refreshing breeze swept through me as the ground leveled below my feet.

Come on, Selena. You're almost there.

Rough, cracked ground scraped my feet as I followed the mesmerizing voice. I walked faster, the pain in my legs feeling all too real, until I reached the edge of a waterfall.

The crystal water rushed off the edge into the pool only a few meters below it. I suddenly felt very warm, the water tempting me to join its descent.

I hesitated, not sure I wanted to jump.

Don't worry. It's a short drop. You'll be fine. Aren't you hot? Don't you want to cool off? The voice asked. He was very wise; I couldn't help but agree with him.

"Yes," I whispered.

All you have to do is jump.

"Yes," I repeated. I took a step up to the ledge, ready to plunge down into the refreshing, glistening water below. The wind blew through my hair, caressing me, teasing me, challenging me to jump. I bent my knees, ready to spring.

"Selena!" Something slammed into me, pulling me back from the cliff's edge. Landing on my back, something restrained me, but I couldn't see what it was. I tried to move, but my arms were pinned to my sides.

"Selena, wake up!" A familiar voice yelled in my ear. This voice I didn't fear. "Goddamn it, wake up!"

The waterfall in front of me abruptly vanished. Instead I saw Lexi standing a few feet in front of me, her arms spread out as if she were getting ready to block me, or tackle me. Confusion consumed me. Where was I? I looked down and saw strong arms hold me, familiar hands clasped around my waist. I was lying on Tristan, and he was holding me against him.

"What the hell?" I asked. Lexi relaxed her stance and let out a sigh of relief.

"What were you doing, Selena?" Tristan growled in my ear.

"I'm... not sure," I answered. "Can I get up?" Tristan waited a moment before reluctantly loosening his hold. I stood and took in my surroundings. I was on the roof of a building, Lexi stood in front of the ledge, and Tristan stood behind me. I took a step forward and only managed to see the road many stories below before Lexi blocked my path.

"What are you doing?" I asked, still disoriented.

"What are *you* doing?" Lexi countered angrily.

"I don't understand," I whispered and turned to Tristan for clarification. His expression made me swallow hard. His face was contorted in fear and anger. I took a step back from him. "Why am I up here? And where is here?"

"You're on the roof of the hotel, Selena," Tristan answered.

"How did I get here?" I searched my memory but came up blank.

"You were sleepwalking," Lexi answered.

"No… I was having a dream." I suddenly remembered. I told them what I had seen, and we were able to match my dream with the reality.

"Those barriers you pushed through must have been the doors, the room door, stairwell door and roof door," Tristan started, "That hill you climbed was actually fifteen flights of stairs, and that waterfall you were so tempted to jump down was this." He pointed to the ledge.

"You were standing on that when we got up here," Lexi explained, "Tristan had to pull you back so you wouldn't fall, or jump, or whatever you were doing. If he hadn't heard the room door close, we would have never known you were gone." She shook her head.

"We didn't know where you were going, and I had no idea you were sleepwalking or I would have been faster in chasing you up the stairs," Tristan said. "We just followed, thinking you were going to get some air, but when I saw you walking toward the ledge…" He ground his teeth.

"Yeah, well we know what happened then," Lexi finished.

"I could have died. I could have jumped off this building, killing myself, because of a dream. How did this happen?" I asked stunned.

"One guess," Lexi answered angrily.

"Darien," Tristan snarled.

"Why does he keep torturing me?" I yelled. Tristan's face, which was a mask of anger, softened, and he rubbed my arm comfortingly.

"Like I told you before, he's trying to scare you and mess with your head." Tristan said. I started shaking as the fear and reality slammed into me. Tears pooled in my eyes, making the rooftop blur. I looked up to prevent them from falling, but I couldn't. Tristan stood by me, still rubbing my arm, but Lexi grabbed me and hugged me tight. I cried into her shirt and she let me. I was just so tired.

Tristan and Lexi let me cry myself out and then they led me toward the stairwell. My ankle protested at having been so overly used, and I whimpered at the pain.

"How did you manage to get all this way without your crutches?" Tristan asked as an afterthought.

"I barely felt it in my dream," I answered.

"I just assumed your ankle was better since you were moving so easily. I should have known." He closed his eyes and took a deep breath, steadying his self-directed anger.

"Don't do that," I said.

"Do what?" Tristan asked, opening his eyes and letting the sun reflect off the yellow specks.

"Feel guilty. It was a messed up thing to happen, but no one was hurt. You did your job; you protected me, even if it was delayed by your standards. Just let it go," I said softly.

Tristan was speechless. He opened his mouth to say something, but closed it again.

I took another step, but couldn't manage the pain. Tristan scooped me up in his arms and carried me down the stairs. I repressed the urge to smile.

By the time we reached our room, I was in shock with how far I had gone, all under the pretense of a dream. It was terrifyingly amazing.

I crawled into bed, pulled the covers up to my chin and stared at the ceiling trying to absorb what just happened. Was I not going through enough crap already? Did I really need Darien messing with my mind on top of it all? I resisted the urge to cry again, not wanting to fall into the self-pity that was hovering around me. I closed my eyes and tried to block out all the negative thoughts.

Lexi didn't have a problem sleeping next to me this time. She crawled into the bed and lay close to me. Tristan checked the wrap on my ankle before re-icing it. Then he sat on his bed stiffly and I knew it would be a while before he let this go.

"Glad to see you're staying in the room, Romeo," Lexi said, shooting a glare at Tristan whose eyes blazed with anger.

"Shut up, Lex," Tristan said through gritted teeth. Lexi only rolled her eyes. I closed mine.

"Can you two just get along please? I have had enough negativity for a lifetime without you two fighting," I said.

"We're not fighting," Lexi started. "I was merely making a statement. That's all. If Tristan wants to get all butt-hurt about it, that's his problem."

Tristan's shoulders bunched tight. "I am not butt-hurt. I just want you to shut up."

"Whatever," Lexi mumbled. I let out a sigh.

"There are more important things right now," I said as my eyes sprang open, "like say, oh I don't know, Darien almost killing me." Tristan stood and started pacing.

"Why is he trying to kill you?" Lexi asked, deep in thought. "He stripped your powers, why go through all this?"

"Could we be getting close?" I asked, daring to hope. "Maybe he knows we're close to unbinding my powers, and he's scared." The thought made me smile.

"Could be," Lexi said.

"We need to keep looking!" I sat up in bed, suddenly feeling alert.

"Easy there, Grasshopper," Lexi said, pushing me back down. "We will. Obviously we're doing something right."

"Whatever the reason, we need to protect you better." Tristan shot a look at Lexi, "*We* need to protect her better, Lex."

"I know," she agreed, letting out a sigh of her own. "I got it! I will put an alarm spell on the door at night, so if it opens, we'll be alerted." She beamed.

"Sounds good to me." I yawned, my momentary energy burst dissolving as quickly as it came. Lexi jumped out of bed to cast the spell and Tristan resumed his stiff posture on his bed.

"We have to do more." Tristan walked to me and let his hands hover around my head. I knew he was recasting his own spell, one that would protect my mind. "I'm sorry," he whispered when he was finished.

"Don't be. I'm fine, thanks to you and Lexi. You need to relax and get some rest."

Tristan sighed, stood and rummaged through his pants.

"Selena, there's something I want you to have, but I don't want you to read into it. It's strictly for protection." He pulled out a box from his pocket and gave it to me.

"After tonight, you need it more than ever," he explained. I opened the box and found the most beautiful necklace I had ever seen. It was a huge pear-cut amethyst hanging off an intricately entwined silver chain.

"Wow," I whispered, admiring the stone. I moved my hair over my shoulder and let it fall down my side. I wrapped the necklace around my neck and tried to clasp it. My fingers kept slipping, and after a moment I looked to Tristan for help. He gave me a half smile before coming to the bed and taking the chain ends from me. He clasped it easily, and I felt the weight of the pendant on my chest. There was a slight tingling on my skin where the stone touched it, and it was comforting.

"You didn't think to give this to me before I got mind-attacked by Darien?" I teased. Tristan's jaw clenched.

"I should have. I'm sorry."

"I'm just kidding, there was no way you could've known what was going to happen. The fact you got me anything at all is surprising. Thank you."

"Again with the thanking. It's just for your protection. Now rest."

I smiled at Tristan.

Tristan nodded, took a deep breath and forced himself in bed. Lexi came back a moment later, turned off the light and crawled in bed beside me.

I hadn't even realized I fell asleep again until I woke up to Lexi speaking loudly.

"You seriously have issues, do you know that?" I heard her say.

"Lexi, just mind your own business. You're making way too big a deal out of this."

"You're just a stupid boy. She could have died! Is that not incentive enough?"

"Oh my God. Get off my back. I will deal with this however I want to. You have no say in this matter. And if I didn't sleep on the couch, we may not have known she was out there!"

"Yeah? Well if you *didn't* sleep on the couch you would have known Selena was sleepwalking. Instead you assumed she left because she was mad you didn't sleep next to her."

"Let this go, Lexi," Tristan growled.

"She's my best friend. She deserves-"

"Can you two please. Shut. Up!" I yelled.

"What?" I heard Lexi ask confused. "Did you have a link to her?"

"I didn't think I did, but somewhere along the way I must have."

"What? What is it now? Please, I'm so tired," I whined from my bed. I reluctantly opened my eyes. Lexi and Tristan had been standing by the window and turned to face me.

"Selena, we weren't talking out loud," Tristan said. "We were speaking telepathically. I must have opened a link to you, I'm sorry, I didn't mean to wake you."

"Huh? But it sounded so real."

"Yeah, it does that." Lexi chuckled. "Why are you so tired? You've been sleeping for eight hours."

"Ew, it's…" I did the math, "one in the afternoon?" I asked. Tristan and Lexi nodded. "I don't know; I just want to sleep."

Tristan looked at Lexi intently and then back at me. "Well aside from Darien's taunting, I think you might be tired because the binding is starting to drain you."

"What do you mean?"

"The binding strips a witch of her powers, and once there are no more powers to strip, it starts to strip away at the witch herself. It's getting your energy," Tristan explained.

"Great," I grumbled.

"How's your ankle?" he asked.

"I don't know. You check it, I'll sleep." I stuck my feet out from under the covers. Tristan and Lexi both laughed.

"Get up!" Lexi yelled in my ear. I rubbed at it reflexively.

"I promise I will if you get me coffee."

"I'm on it." Lexi jumped up and off, out of the room. I got out of bed and washed up, before sitting in the living room area. Tristan unwrapped my ankle and checked the swelling. Once he was content with what he saw, he wrapped it up and iced it again for me.

Lexi came in with my coffee and the aroma hit me and woke up my senses.

"Thank you!" I took the coffee and savored it. "So which cemetery are we going to tonight?"

"Well," Lexi looked down at the map still on the table. "We can go to the one on Laughlin; it's the next closest one."

"Okay. At least we don't have to bring any shovels this time." I smiled. "Hey, if Tristan does his invisibility thing, can't we go in the daytime instead of night?"

"For starters, I don't make you invisible, I make you unnoticed. Secondly, there are visitors in the day, and people will see us if they get close enough, or pay enough attention. So I would rather not risk it."

"Fine. Oh, speaking of spells." I turned to Lexi. "I was thinking, my ankle got hurt because it was sucked in the ground that was under a spell. If you undid the effects of the spell on my foot, do you think it would work?"

"Actually, Genevieve and Lachlan should be here soon," Tristan said. I nodded, anxious to have full use of my ankle again.

"I could try anyway," Lexi said. "Whether it works or not depends on if it was the ground that hurt you, or Tristan when he physically tried to free you," she answered, reaching for my foot. I lifted it up and she unwrapped it. She studied the bluish, purple bruising and swelling and then she placed her tiny hands on my ankle. She held them there for a moment concentrating. She opened her eyes and when she saw that my foot hadn't changed, a look of disappointment crossed her face.

"I'm sorry, Selena. It won't work."

"It's okay. At least you tried." I smiled at her reassuringly. It was a long shot anyway. I started rewrapping my foot.

"Here, I can do that," Tristan said, a look of guilt on his face.

"It's okay, I feel bad you guys are all over my foot." I laughed. "Are you okay?" I asked Tristan, turning serious. He nodded.

"I'm just sorry I was the one who hurt your ankle," he said, looking down at my hands as I rewrapped my swollen joint.

"Really? You're feeling bad about this? You saved my life—twice in one day actually—who cares if I sprained something in the process. Look at the bigger picture," I said finishing up the wrap. I thought I did a decent job until Tristan sighed and lifted my foot onto his lap and redid it.

We sat quietly for a moment and then my stomach growled. "You up for lunch?" I asked sheepishly.

Lexi nodded, "Yeah, I'm starving. We should eat and gather our strength. Tonight's going to be another long one." Lexi stood and was out the door in a flash.

We sat and waited the rest of the time in silence until Lexi returned carrying sub sandwiches. Shortly after we finished eating there was a knock on the door. Tristan went to open it, and Genevieve and Lachlan walked in. We greeted each other while Tristan locked the door behind them.

I hadn't seen them since we killed Crystal and Yuri. It was nice seeing them again, but it reminded of me of the one thing I'd been working hard to forget.

Genevieve looked down at my ankle then and took in a breath.

"Oh, you poor thing. Here, let me help you. That is why I'm here after all," she said excitedly. She had my bandage off so fast I didn't even feel it. Then she placed her hands over my ankle and closed her eyes. I felt a warm, tingling sensation, and then a pressure on my foot that made me scrunch up my face in pain. I watched my ankle and saw the swelling slowly go down, and then the bruising faded until my normal skin color returned.

I gasped in relief. Genevieve opened her eyes. "I still can't get over how great it is to heal people." She shone. I heard Lexi let out a sigh.

I stood up tentatively and slowly put pressure on my leg. It was perfectly fine.

"Thank you." I hugged Genevieve. "I'm sorry you had to come all this way for something so minor. Are you alright? Do you feel tired now?" I hated that healing me would make Genevieve weak.

"I'm fine. It didn't require much energy at all. Besides, your well-being is nothing minor, and it's not like we had to travel far; we live here," Genevieve said.

"Oh, is this what you meant when you said you lived close to Vegas?" I asked, remembering asking Genevieve something similar in Arizona. She was very vague then.

"Yes, I didn't want to overwhelm you with information about The Hidden City when you were so new to magic. Our cottage is here so I spell-crafted the half-way house in Arizona to be closer to you." She smiled.

"Wow, well thank you again."

"It's my pleasure," she replied, making me feel like unworthy royalty. "But if you don't mind me asking, why didn't you just heal yourself?"

We all went quiet.

Should we tell them? I heard Tristan's voice in my head.

If you think they can be trusted. Lexi responded.

It felt good to be involved in a silent conversation for once, and yet I said, *Doesn't matter to me.* I made sure to direct my thought to Tristan only. I think it worked, not that it mattered, but it was good to practice.

"Do we have your complete trust?" Tristan asked his friends out loud.

"Of course," Genevieve answered.

"Well," Tristan started, "Remember when I saw you before and you told me you heard rumors that Darien weakened Selena?"

I flinched at that. Had Darien been telling people that? It made my blood boil to think of him gloating about it.

Genevieve and Lachlan nodded. "Well it's true. He found a way to bind her powers," Tristan finished. Their jaws dropped, and then panic flashed in their eyes.

"Hell," Lachlan said, running his hand over his face. "We have to figure something out so we can deal with Darien once and for all." And then he glanced at Tristan, "Sorry," he mumbled, his Scottish accent punctuating the words.

"Where is Darien during all of this now?" Genevieve asked.

"That's what worries me," Tristan answered. "We don't know where he is, and I have a bad feeling he's up to something none of us are expecting."

"Other than trying to kill me?" I asked, repressing a shudder.

Tristan sighed, a frown creeping across his face.

"So what do we do?" Genevieve asked.

"There's nothing to be done once you're rebound." Lachlan shook his head.

"Actually, we're working on that," Lexi answered.

Genevieve and Lachlan stayed silent, waiting for the rest.

"We were told that-" I started, but my tongue suddenly felt three sizes too big. "We can," my tongue became cement in my mouth.

"Ah, I see you've been sworn to secrecy." Lachlan chuckled. Huh, so I guess that's what happens when you try to tell the secret. When my mind was sure I wasn't going to say anymore, my tongue returned to normal.

"That's alright. We don't need details; just tell us how we can help," Genevieve offered.

"Well, we are going to a cemetery tonight to find," Tristan spoke tentatively, waiting for the bind to kick in. When he was sure he was okay he continued, "something."

Lexi pulled out her phone, tapped and swiped the screen and then frowned.

"The cl-" Lexi started, then shook her head. "My notes are gone." The wall was blank where she had projected the riddle the day before, as was the sheet of paper she had written it on. "God, he's good."

Lachlan shrugged. "No matter, we're in," he said.

Lexi, Tristan and I looked at each other.

"Thank you," I said.

"Lexi has been casting a detection spell to find this thing. It's enchanted," Tristan managed to say before being stopped. "We had a plan that I would use earth magic to dig the sites where Lexi found something. If you two can manage the same thing, we will be able to finish in half the time."

"Yes, I can do a detection spell, no problem," Genevieve confirmed.

"And I can control the earth," Lachlan added.

"Perfect. We'll leave after sunset," Lexi planned.

And that was exactly what we did. It was well past sunset by the time we reached the cemetery. Genevieve and Lachlan had no idea what they were looking for, but then again, neither did we. This cemetery was smaller than the first; there were no tombs or crypts, only a plot with headstones.

It seemed to be an older cemetery as well, and less visited as weeds grew throughout and onto the worn stone slabs. Tristan searched with Genevieve while Lexi searched with Lachlan. I popped in wherever I was needed. We still spent hours searching, digging, burying and repeating that over and over. I would help occasionally by jumping into the graves, and felt I really took one for the team by doing so. Fortunately, we didn't come across any booby-trapped graves. Unfortunately, after hours of searching, we found nothing. Genevieve and Lachlan went home, defeated like the rest of us, while Tristan, Lexi and I went back to the hotel.

"What if we're making a mistake and wasting our time?" I asked.

"It's possible, but we have no other leads right now," Tristan answered. "I just have a feeling we're on the right track."

"Me too," Lexi said as we walked into the hotel room. "Especially with Darien acting out the way he did."

Tristan locked the door behind us, and Lexi jumped into the shower first again. I took off my boots and went to sit on the bed when the room swayed. The bed and night-stand slanted unnaturally, blurred and refocused. This feeling was unfortunately familiar, but it didn't prevent me from being scared.

"Not again," I said and found the bed before I lost my balance.

"What is it?" Tristan asked coming to my side.

"I think it's another vision or warning. I'm not sure which." I had received a mental warning by some unknown man a few weeks ago. He warned us that Crystal and Yuri were going to attack us, and we survived the ambush because of him.

Selena, the man said in my mind.

"Yep, it's another one." My panic spiked as I wondered what he would tell me now.

Run.

"Where? Why?" I asked aloud.

Run.

"Tell me what's happening." I demanded.

But there was only silence.

"What did you hear?" Tristan asked anxiously.

"He just told me to run, but I have no idea why."

Tristan strode to the bathroom and banged on the door. "Lexi get out of there."

"What is your problem?" She yelled back.

"Selena got a warning. We have to leave."

The water shut off and Lexi ran out of the bathroom dripping wet and wrapped in a towel.

"What warning?"

"He just said run," I repeated, throwing on my boots and lacing them as quickly as possible.

"Who? Run where?" Lexi asked, managing to get dressed without losing her towel.

"We don't know, but I don't want to risk being here," Tristan answered

"This is crazy! What if it's Darien trying to lure you out?" Lexi asked as she put on her shoes.

That made Tristan pause. "How sure are you that it was the same man as before?" Tristan asked me.

"Pretty sure, I mean it felt and sounded the same, but then again Darien has a way of messing with my head, so I can't be certain."

"Shit," Tristan hissed as he ran his hand through his hair trying to decide what to do.

"Listen," Lexi started calmly now. "We are in a protected hotel; no one can get in here, so we have nothing to run from... right? Let's just think this through for a minute."

As Lexi spoke a light flashed in my peripheral and I turned to see what it was, but nothing was there. Then another flash went off in the corner of the room, and then a slew of tiny flashes flickered there.

"Guys..." I said and Tristan and Lexi turned to face me. "No one can get in here but what about that?" My voice trembled with fear. In the corner of the room, where the flashes had been, now stood two… things. I think dogs would best describe them, but they each had three heads, six legs and two tails.

"Is that-" Lexi started as she backed away from the creatures.

"Braktus," Tristan finished, and I remembered him telling me about this creature at the Aracali ruins.

"I guess that part of the story was true," I whispered, slowly backing up toward Tristan and Lexi.

"Yep," Tristan said. The creatures stared at us, white foamy saliva dripping from their jaws, sharp white teeth flashed as they growled, their thick black fur standing on end. Their heads dipped, their tails flicked and numerous paws crept forward.

"Oh… I understand now," I said.

"What?" Lexi asked.

"Run."

14. JAIL TIME

We turned in unison and ran through the door just as the dogs began to spring. We managed to close the bedroom door before the brakti could reach us, but just barely. They scraped their claws against the wood, throwing their weight onto the door and howling.

"How the hell could they get in?" Lexi asked.

"I don't know," Tristan answered. "But we need to move now!" We ran out of the hotel room, down the stairwell, and through the lobby, where Lexi and Tristan practically threw the keys at the clerk, and out the front door.

"Won't the others be in danger of those things?" I asked as we ran.

"No," Tristan said, taking my hand to help me run faster. "Brakti are hunting dogs, they only go after the person they were sent for."

"So someone actually sent that creature after the Princess of Aracali?" I asked, thinking back to the story Tristan told me.

"I don't know, Selena," Tristan yelled, "Can you focus please?" We ran down the street and around the corner.

"Where are we going?" Lexi asked.

"To the Charge station," Tristan answered and started running with renewed purpose. "The safest one is linked to the prison."

"How does that make it the safest?" I asked.

"It's the most protected building in the city," Tristan yelled back to me. Lexi matched his speed, while I was getting pulled behind Tristan like a tube tied to a speed boat. Just then I was suddenly pushed, pulled and twisted as Tristan teleported me to the back of a building.

"Stay right here," Tristan said, pointing to the ground for emphasis, and then vanished. A moment later he re-appeared with Lexi.

We rounded a three-story concrete building, with small windows interspersed throughout and a wall of metal poles, spaced at least two feet apart, surrounding it.

"What are those?" I asked, pointing to the rows of poles surrounding the building.

"It's a fence," Lexi answered as we jogged to the front doors. "Well, it works like a fence by preventing any of the inmates from escaping. See once an inmate is checked in here, they get a spell placed on them that would trigger the fences if they get too close."

"What would happen if they did?" I asked.

"They would get shocked unconscious and teleported to their cell," Tristan answered.

"Are there a lot of people in prison here?"

"Not everyone gets their powers bound as a sentence for their crimes," Tristan said. "Most get locked away in an anti-power cell."

Lexi opened the door, and Tristan and I walked through first. The lobby was a small room with cobblestone floors, grey walls, and a desk that two Charge officers sat behind. The desk was surprisingly open, no cages or glass protectors, though I was sure a magic barrier was in place.

"What seems to be the problem, folks?" one of the officers asked. He had short black curly hair and a mustache that would have made Tom Selleck jealous. His belly protruded in front of him, making me wonder if there was a spell for weight loss.

"We need access-" Tristan started, but the other officer cut him off.

"Little late to be wandering around the prison, isn't it?" He asked, getting to his feet. This officer was tall and lean, his blond hair cropped in a military crew cut.

"We need a safe place," Lexi said.

"From what?" The tall officer stood quickly.

"Someone sent brakti after us," Tristan explained, looking over his shoulder at the night outside.

"Brakti?" The mustached officer laughed. "Those are mythological."

"Officer Hal, is it?" I asked reading his name tag. He huffed. "You live in The Hidden City, a place where only witches live, and you're telling me you can't believe that a mythological creature could actually exist?" I asked stunned.

His face reddened, "Well, I'm sorry, but we can't help you."

"Unless you want us to arrest you," the tall officer teased.

"I'm sure you folks'll be fine, just head on home," Hal said.

Some Charge! I was so angry that they didn't believe us. Something slammed against the glass doors and made us all jump. The officers' mouths dropped as they looked outside. Tristan, Lexi and I spun around to see what was out there. Sure enough the two brakti were throwing their distorted bodies against the glass.

"It's impossible," Hal said under his breath. Again, I was baffled at his closed-mindedness when he was a witch living in a magical city! "Brent, are you seeing this?"

"Come back here," the tall officer, Brent, said, ushering us behind the desk. He waved his hands at the glass door and a blue light shone along the surface, sealing itself. I recognized the protective spell, since Lexi had done it a few times.

The slamming continued for a few moments before everything became deathly quiet. I dropped to all fours and crept out from behind the desk to get a better look through the front doors.

"Get back here," Tristan hissed.

"I'm not going outside; I just want to see--" The area outside was completely deserted, no crazy mutated dogs, but the area directly in front of me, right in the lobby, was starting to flash, like a thousand cameras going off at once. In an instant the two brakti materialized a breathing distance away from me. Their hot, rank breath reached me, and I froze in place as the creatures crept forward. The numerous heads swiveled back and forth, but all six pairs of eyes never left my face. The tails twitched and flicked, revealing sharp pointed ends, as their claws scraped noisily on the stone.

I felt a tug on my ankle, but was too scared to look away from the creatures pursuing me.

"Crawl backwards," Tristan urgently hissed.

I slowly moved my left leg back, and then the right, trying not to make any sudden movements. It didn't matter, the brakti snarled and pounced. Tristan grabbed my ankle and jerked me back to him as Hal sent an electric bolt to shock one of the creatures. It jerked as the current hit it, and fell to the ground.

Lexi threw up her sphere shield to protect us and Brent shot fireballs at the second braktus, setting its coarse fur ablaze. The creature whimpered and wailed like a dog in pain, and I had a sudden urge to help it. I was about to step forward when the braktus charged at me. Tristan pulled me behind him just as the braktus threw itself at the force field, searing one of its heads on impact. Whimpering, the creature flickered and vanished.

The braktus that had been stunned now came to, and was pacing in front of our safety bubble.

Lexi forced the shield out so it would hit the braktus and maim it too, but it moved back just out of reach before it flashed and disappeared.

"Where did it go?" I asked, tentatively stepping forward.

"I don't know, but it will be back," Tristan answered, pulling me behind him again. "Is there any way you can let us into the holding cell area? The protective charms are the strongest there, aren't they?"

The officers exchanged a glance as if this were some unknown secret.

"Follow me," Hal finally said. He led us through a heavy metal door that he had to swipe his hand in front of to open.

"Will it matter if we're in the cell area?" Lexi asked. "I mean they got in the building already."

"How did it cross the protective spells?" Hal asked, still a little shaken.

"It's not possible," Brent answered.

"It got through the hotel's safety wards too," Lexi said. "Maybe they have some kind of bypass spell that allows them to get in anywhere."

"No, those are ancient creatures that cannot be bound by certain protective charms," Tristan said. "Whoever sent them knew that."

"Like Darien?" Lexi asked.

The Charge shifted uncomfortably, and I realized they probably had no idea who we were.

"Well then what's the point of going deeper in the building?" I asked.

"Because the spells cast in the holding cells are just as ancient," Tristan explained. "I can't guarantee it will stop the brakti, but it's our best shot."

We walked down two hallways and through three security doors before we reached the cells. They looked almost like human prison cells, except there were no locks, just metal poles lined from ceiling to floor, two feet apart, like the outer fence.

As we walked through this area, the first few cells were empty, but as we went deeper, witches filled the cells, some containing three or more. They called to us, begging for freedom and escape. They didn't get close to the bars, or stick their arms out like they do in the movies, but we could hear their cries from the back of their cells. They all wore white jumpsuits that looked impeccably clean in contrast to the inmates' shaggy state. Most of them had long, unkempt hair and beards and looked malnourished.

"Are these poles like the outer fence, where they could get shocked?" I asked.

Hal looked at me as if I should already know this, "Yes," he answered shortly. I had other questions but decided to keep them to myself. Or maybe I could just ask Tristan telepathically.

Tristan looked at me then and smiled.

Where are the women? And don't they feed them here? I asked Tristan.

Women are on a different floor, and they feed them just enough to sustain them, but keep them too weak to escape, he answered.

We walked through another hallway and into a room with a table and four chairs around it.

"Where are we?" I asked, forgetting to keep my questions to myself.

"Visiting room," Brent answered.

"We should be safe here," Tristan said. "Theoretically."

"Great," I mumbled. The officers took two of the seats, and Lexi took another while Tristan and I paced.

"If this works, and we're safe here, how long will we have to stay?" I asked.

"I don't know, let's just find out if it will even work," Tristan answered.

"Shouldn't you guys get other officers to cover your station? And maybe help us out here?" Lexi asked.

"Our station is taken care of, and we will not waste any more resources on brakti," Hal said.

Tristan spun suddenly, and we all turned to the back of the room where Tristan was looking. The flashes began again and my stomach dropped. Damn these things were persistent.

Lexi jumped up and created her sphere shield as the guards left their seats to join Tristan and I behind it. The brakti emerged as I suspected it would, only what I didn't expect was for there to be three of them this time, including the one with the seared head. Its neck hung limp, the head charred, showing the bone beneath the burned flesh, a melted mass of black hanging from the creature's body.

"What the shit?" Brent asked.

"So much for theoretically," Lexi said. Instead of pouncing like I thought they would, the brakti paced in front of us, inching closer with each turn, until one stopped and looked straight at us. It opened its jaws and started speaking. I shook my head in surprise.

"Tristan, you're so fond of fairytales," the braktus said, but it was Darien's voice that came out. "Tell our precious Selena what happened to the Aracali Princess when the braktus attacked." The Charge stiffened and looked at me, I guess they knew who I was now.

Tristan stayed silent.

"Don't be shy, Tristan. Tell her or I will kill that fat chut," the braktus said swinging one of its heads to face Hal.

"You can't get past the shield, Darien," Lexi said to the mutated dog.

"No, but I can make him come out," he said. Hal's eyes lost focus, and he began to sway drunkenly. "Unless you want to test that, Tristan, tell her."

"She knows the Aracali Princess survived," Tristan finally answered.

"Yes, but tell her how," the braktus ordered.

"Because it's said that Teague sent the braktus himself to trick the princess into trusting him, and only the witch who sent the braktus has the power to stop it."

"Very good," the braktus said. Hal's eyes refocused and he shook his head to clear the effects of Darien's spell.

"Now that you know your chances of survival are non-existent, I suggest you listen to me very carefully. I can call off the hounds, if you give me Selena."

"Over my dead body," Tristan snarled.

"Well, obviously," the braktus said. "That's what we're negotiating here, isn't it? Your lives. So what will it be? Four lives for the price of one? Or five deaths?"

The officers shifted, and looked at us uncertainly.

"Don't hurt anyone," I said, stepping forward. Tristan grabbed my wrist.

"Smart girl, Selena," the braktus said.

"No," Tristan snarled.

"I can't let anyone get killed because of me. It's not worth it."

"The hell it isn't," Hal spoke up and stepped out of the protective sphere.

"No," I cried as he charged at the braktus, sparks flying from his fingers and showering the creature. It writhed and went down just as the other two charged. They leaped at Hal as Brent set one braktus on fire. The other sunk its teeth into Hal's arm, his screams filling the small room. Brent spun and began to cast a spell to force the creature off his partner, just as the two-headed braktus pounced, taking Brent down. Tristan swept his arms open, sending a gust of wind to push the brakti back. The braktus gripping Hal refused to release him, shaking his body from side to side. I rushed to Hal, wanting to help, but having no idea how. Before I reached him, Tristan grabbed my arm, pulling back.

"We have to help him!" I yelled.

Tristan looked at me sternly. "Don't leave Lexi's shield." He pushed me back and physically tried prying the braktus off Hal as Brent got to his feet, charring the other braktus, but unable to kill it. Tristan tried wrapping his arms around the braktus' torso, but one of the heads released Hal, and spun to attack Tristan, biting his shoulder. "Tristan!" I screamed as he cried out in pain and released his hold. Staggering back Tristan looked to Lexi, unsure of what to do.

"Get behind me," Lexi ordered as she expanded her shield out. The other braktus pounced on Hal as Lexi's shield reached the creatures, searing whatever limbs it touched. The brakti yelped and released Hal long enough for Tristan to pull him behind the shield. Brent knelt down to tend to Hal's wounds.

"Darien!" Tristan snarled.

"Yes," one braktus said, as the other two fell back, pacing behind him. "Are you ready to make that deal?"

"Yes!" I yelled, as Tristan said, "No!"

We glared at each other, and the braktus laughed.

"Call them off," Tristan ordered.

The braktus tilted one of its heads quizzically. "Now, why would I do that?"

"Please," I said, wanting to step forward, but knowing that Tristan would stop me. "Please, stop this."

I got an idea, Lexi said. *Keep talking.*

"Selena," the braktus said. "I have you all exactly where I want you, why would I stop?"

Tristan shifted next to Lexi, and Brent stood on her other side.

"Because you know you don't want to do this. If you kill us, you won't get to complete your ritual."

"You forget, I can kill them and leave you alive to suffer their loss."

I swallowed back a sob. Lexi's shield crept out slowly in front of us, but it seemed the braktus didn't see it.

"I won't help you," I said, lifting my chin. "You think you can kill the people I love and still expect me to help with some stupid ritual? As soon as you gave me my powers I'd kill you." Venom seeped in my voice.

Before the braktus could respond the shield sprung out, at first searing the creatures' fur, then flesh, muscles, bones, until there was nothing left of them but ash, and the echoes of their cries.

The room was quiet, the dogs vanished. Hal's whimpering was the only noise. Lexi and Brent knelt by the injured officer.

"Hang on," Lexi said, holding her hands over Hal's wounds. He lay on the floor, torn flesh on the left side of his body, blood pooling around him. A moment later, Lexi cried out in frustration. "Braktus are magical creatures, their bites are spelled, so I should be able to reverse the damage they cause, but it's not working!"

"He's too injured," Brent said quietly.

"We need to get out of here," I said. "Tristan, teleport him to a hospital!"

"I can't teleport out of the prison," He answered sadly, shaking his head.

"Then carry him and we'll run!"

"No," Hal coughed. I knelt down beside him.

"You'll be okay," I said through tears. "You have to be."

"Tell my son," Hal started, barely whispering, "that I love him. Tell him that I died..." He coughed, weak and wet, and blood flecked his lips. "Tell him I died protecting the chosen."

"Saving the world," Tristan added softly, and Hal nodded almost imperceptibly before he shut his eyes, his head falling limp.

"No!" I cried. I shook him, wanting him to wake up. He couldn't have died for me! My thoughts were an angry yelling voice in my head. Not for me! I cried over this courageous man's body; hot angry tears.

"Selena," Tristan whispered, pulling me up. My hands and knees were covered in Hal's blood, and it was all my fault.

"I'm sorry," I whispered, first to Hal, then to Brent who stood frozen, staring at his partner. "I'm so sorry."

Brent nodded.

"You should go," Brent said.

I shook my head, but Tristan was already pulling me away. I shook myself free of Tristan's hold and ran to Brent, hugging him.

"Thank you." I held him a moment longer, before releasing him. Again he nodded.

"Tristan," Lexi said, "take Selena outside. I'll help Brent."

"No," Brent said. "We have protocol for a fallen officer. There's nothing you can do here. I'll let you out."

Reluctantly we left, following Brent out of the prison, heads down.

"Your shoulder," I said to Tristan. Blood soaked his shirt.

"I'll be fine," he said gruffly. I wanted to scream. If I had my powers, I would have been able to save Hal, heal Tristan, destroy Darien. Darien... I hated him.

Brent led us outside without another word, and I felt it; the guilt, his and my own. I'm sure he blamed me for what happened to Hal, after all, I blamed myself.

"Will Darien send brakti to our room again?" I asked before Tristan teleported us back.

"Not likely," Tristan answered.

"Why not?"

"He knows we can defeat them now," Tristan answered.

"How did you guys kill them, by the way?"

"Lexi had the idea that our collective powers would make the shield lethal."

"I will re-seal the room anyway," Lexi said.

"Good," Tristan said as he took my hand and teleported me back to the hotel.

We got to our room, and as promised, Lexi sealed it, but this time the blue shimmer stayed in place.

"You want me to fix that?" Lexi asked, pointing to Tristan's shoulder.

"No," he said. "I deserve much worse."

"So… what?" Lexi asked. "This is your penance for not saving Hal?"

Tristan stiffened. "It's not that bad. It won't hinder me, so just leave it alone."

Lexi nodded.

I went to the bathroom and wet a towel.

"At least let me clean it," I said, walking back into the room.

Tristan sighed and removed his shirt. Dried blood caked around his neck and down his chest. He sat on the edge of the bed and I gently wiped around the wound. Thankfully the bleeding had almost stopped. I managed to clean most of the wound and was cleaning the blood off his chest when Tristan grabbed my wrist. I looked up to see him studying me.

"Were you really going to go with Darien?" He asked.

"Yes," I answered honestly.

"Why?"

"Because right now I'm no good to anybody. I'm damaged goods. I have no powers, I can't save anyone, and maybe this was my purpose. Maybe my appeasing Darien would distract him from hurting anyone else."

"Selena, you can't think like that," Tristan said, releasing his hold.

"Well, I do." I stared down at the blood soaked towel in my hands. "Hal died for me."

"Any one of us would," Tristan said.

"Whether you believe it or not," Lexi said, "you are amazing, and you are important."

"I'm not!" I yelled stepping away from Tristan. "I hate that people are so willing to believe in me and I don't even have any powers! He had a son; a boy who will grow up without a father because of me."

"His son will be proud," Tristan said, standing up. "His father believed in you, and so do I."

"Me too, babe," Lexi said.

"You are both crazy," I said. "Say what you want, but I still think I should give myself up to Darien. Keep everyone else safe."

"Listen to me," Tristan said. "Darien may promise you things, but he's not to be trusted. Believe me when I tell you this; I know from experience."

"What kind of experience?" I asked. "What happened?"

"Nothing I want to get into right now," Tristan said as Lexi shot him a glare. "When I warned you about him before your date, was I wrong?"

"No," I said. That thing was such a mess, and I thought Tristan was crazy at the time.

"I didn't lie to you then; I won't now. Nothing you do as far as Darien is concerned will make a difference, short of killing him."

"Great," I mumbled. I looked at my clothes, still covered in Hal's blood. "I need to get cleaned up." A sob escaped me as I rushed to the bathroom.

We didn't and couldn't talk about Hal after that. We focused instead on getting my powers back, and making sure that Hal hadn't died in vain.

15. BENEATH THE LIVING IS THE DEAD

Fortunately Darien didn't send any more mutant hounds, unfortunately we weren't getting anywhere with our search. What was even worse, was that during the three nights and cemetery searches that followed, we were still no closer to solving the riddle, or finding the object. Thankfully none of the cemeteries were as big as the first one. We found enchanted bracelets, rings, necklaces, watches, articles of clothing even, but nothing plant-related. I was hoping that we didn't miss it somehow, because, really we weren't sure that we were supposed to be looking for a plant, it just made the most sense. I also really hoped that we were on the right track by searching graves and cemeteries.

After searching through five graveyards, my doubts were seriously heightened. Not to mention, I was down-right exhausted lately. I could feel the spell eating away at me. The more drained I felt, the more worried Lexi and Tristan looked.

Genevieve and Lachlan were wonderful and patient, helping any way they could. The afternoon after our most recent search, we sat in the sitting area of the hotel room, drinking coffee and eating muffins that Lexi bought. We had just woken up, our sleep schedules reversed from being up all night. Our mornings now were mid-day.

We were going over that night's grave-digging plan. I was laying down on the love seat, my feet over Lexi's lap, Tristan sat on the arm chair across from us, Lachlan and Genevieve sat on the couch. They hovered over the map, studying the streets to our next destination.

I pulled a blanket up to my shoulders and pondered my physical state.

Tristan, I sent silently, to his mind. He looked up instinctively, meeting my eyes. *Why am I so drained this time? I never felt anything like this when I was bound before.*

There was so much sadness in Tristan's eyes, it made my heart ache. We had done very well keeping our boundaries, and had been maintaining a professional relationship, but moments like this made me want to throw the rules out the window.

Each time a binding spell is cast on a witch it has a stronger effect. Initially they will be fine, if not sad, but if they are bound more than once, their bodies can't handle it. It's very unusual for a witch to get bound twice, but it does happen. He explained silently. I nodded, feeling a sense of hopelessness before deciding to tune back into the conversation the others were having.

"I think we should go to Alexander Graham Cemetery next," Lexi was saying, pointing to the circle on the map. The name tickled at a memory, but as I grasped for it, it slipped away.

"Well we only have one more after that, so I guess it doesn't matter which one we do at this point," Lachlan said, his accent heightened at certain words. I looked around at the group and saw that they were all tired, sore and losing hope. I felt so bad that they were doing all this for me. I promised myself, if I got better, I would make it up to them somehow.

The rest of the afternoon was uneventful. We ate, rested and then got ready for the next attempt at grave-digging. I was dragging my feet getting dressed.

"Maybe you should stay here tonight," Tristan advised, taking in my weakened state.

"No, I'm okay, really. I just need a second wind," I pushed. He shook his head slightly but didn't argue.

"Do you think she did the right thing?" I whispered to Lexi on the way to the cemetery.

"Who?" she asked. We sat in the back seat, heads close together.

"My mom," I looked down at my hands. "Maybe if she had raised me as a witch I would have been better prepared for this. Maybe I would have known Darien was binding my powers, and I could have stopped him so I wouldn't turn into... this."

"She was protecting you, Selena."

"Was she though? I mean, look at me. Because I was bound before, this second time will probably kill me. Not to mention that I didn't grow up learning how to use my powers, so I had to be taught at twenty-five. That didn't help anyone."

"How could she have known?" Lexi asked. "I know binding your powers was extreme, but it was necessary, and raising you human, although you missed out on basic training, kept you safe. Your mom did what she thought was best, and it worked, if not in the way you imagined."

"Well, I'm not safe now," I said. "I'm a target, and an easy one. I can't save myself, never mind anyone else. I'm running on fumes here."

"I'm sorry this happened," Lexi said, taking my hand. "But you need to trust that we will get through this."

I didn't have the heart to trust anything, but I nodded my head anyway.

We reached Alexander Graham Cemetery then, quietly got out of the car and crept in. Tristan placed his discretion spell and we started our search. The temperature was perfect as always; the waning moon hung overhead, softly lighting our path. There were tombstones in the center of the cemetery surrounded by a row of catacombs. We searched for almost two hours before it dawned on me.

"Guys," I called, ushering to Tristan and Lexi. Genevieve and Lachlan held back, knowing I couldn't tell them what I needed to say. "I think I figured it out," I started once they were within whispering distance. "'The name that goes with bell and bell.' Well I know part of it at least. The cemetery is named Alexander Graham." When I got blank stares from Tristan and Lexi I explained. "You know, Alexander Graham *Bell*? The guy who invented the telephone?" Recognition dawned on their faces then. "I think we are definitely in the right place. We just need to figure out which other name goes with bell, since it was listed twice. Right?" I said enthusiastically.

For the first time in over a week, I saw Lexi and Tristan's faces light up.

"You're brilliant!" Lexi said giving me a quick hug. Tristan stood behind her smiling, but held himself back.

"So we were right to look for headstones with names relating to bell then," Tristan said, walking out toward the headstones.

"Right, just not flower names, I guess." I said.

We continued looking around, reading each name with renewed hope that we hadn't been wasting our time doing that before.

"What's going on?" Lachlan asked curiously.

"Nothing we hadn't already been doing," Tristan started, "Just got confirmation we're on the right track. We found," but when he tried to tell them, the oath of secrecy restricted him.

"Curse this damned spell," Lachlan swore out of frust-ration. "Come on, Gen, let's just keep doin' what we're doin'." They continued looking for anything magically infused, and we carried on looking at the names.

I came across a shared grave, with a very large, white, marble headstone. The writing was engraved in gold, and there were pictures of angels carved on the corners. It was the most beautiful headstone I had ever seen, with dozens of roses and fresh flowers placed beneath it. I read the names and my breath caught.

HERE LIE

| HONORIA ARTURRO | AND | WILLIAM ARTURRO |
| MAY 21, 1962 | | SEPTEMBER 4, 1959 |

TO
AUGUST 15, 1999
BELOVED PARENTS
YOU WILL BE MISSED

I gasped and knelt at their graves. I tried not to cry, but I felt a rogue tear slide down my cheek. The traitor.

"Oh, Selena. I'm so sorry," Tristan whispered behind me.

"I overheard the paramedics say there was nothing left of them, that their bodies were basically cremated from the house fire. I never knew they were buried. There was only a memorial service for them, no coffins, no urns, nothing; just a picture of them, smiling, completely unaware of what was coming." A sob escaped my throat.

Tristan placed his hand on my shoulder. "Witches have a way of covering their tracks. The paramedics could have even been witches. Think about it, your parents wouldn't have been able to explain this place to any human mourners," he said trying to comfort me.

I nodded and wiped at the tears that were now flowing. "I miss them so much; they would know what do." My heart ached for my parents, and the feeling of safety they provided. I always tried to keep my feelings bottled up when it came to my mother and father, but this was too much for me to handle. Especially since I felt so weak.

"Who are all these flowers from?" I asked, taking in the beautiful colors in this dreary place.

"People here believe in you, Selena," Tristan said. "They're showing their respect."

I couldn't believe it. I felt so touched, and yet so scared. I didn't want to let the people of this city down, or my parents. I didn't know what to do.

"It's never easy losing a parent." Tristan was quiet a moment. "Let alone two. I'll leave you alone with them," he said, and I sensed him walk away. I sat there, thinking about them and remembering the happy moments we shared. I talked to them, telling them that I missed and loved them, and that I wished they were here with me. I sent a silent prayer that they help me get through this. I told them that I wished I could have made them proud by being strong and powerful instead of weak and bound. I stayed there for a few more moments in silence.

"Hey, I think I found something," I heard Lexi call. I wiped my tears and regained my composure. I took a deep breath and sent a silent goodbye to my parents. I pushed aside the longing feeling that found its way to my chest and went to see Lexi. Genevieve, Lachlan and Tristan were already there.

"What is it?" I asked, feeling too sad to get excited.

"What does a bell do?" She asked. Her excitement was written all over her face, and she looked like she was about to burst. We all looked at her silently. "It tolls!" She pointed to a large tomb. Above the doorway was the name Benjamin Toll. I felt a smile spread across my face. Genevieve and Lachlan exchanged confused glances.

"This is a good thing I take it?" Genevieve started. "Is this where the object is?"

"We believe so," Tristan answered. Wasting no time, he tried to open the door. When it didn't budge, he started pushing it and using his body weight to pry it open. He placed his hands on the stone door, and a pulse shot through his palms, pushing the door open.

"Gen and I will wait out here," Lachlan told us as we entered the tomb. Inside was stuffy and small. It was a square room with one stained glass window centered on one wall that, when illuminated by the moon, cast a multicolored pattern on the floor.

A cement coffin sat in the center of the room and was engraved with numerous designs. I knew another coffin containing the corpse would be in there, but I wasn't looking forward to trying to open it. In the corner of the room was a wooden table about three feet high. The top six inches looked like solid wood, supported by four wooden legs. On top of the table sat a single rose in a glass of water. It looked like it had recently been placed there, its red petals providing a vibrant color in the moonlight.

Lexi walked over to the rose and gently touched the petals. She shook her head, "This is infused with a minimal amount of magic, just enough to keep it from ever wilting. There must be some other plant-like object around here."

"Do you think it's in the coffin?" I asked, hoping I wouldn't have to dig around in another decaying box. Lexi cast a detection spell.

"No, not in the coffin but…" she let her sentence hang, turning back to the wooden table. She tried the flower again, her eyebrows pulling together in concentration. "I'm sensing there is stronger magic here, but I don't know where it's coming from," Lexi explained. Tristan and I stood next to her, studying the rose and the table.

"Wait," I said suddenly. The moon gave just enough light for me to see an outline of a square in the table top, directly below the rose. I ran my finger along its edge and looked for a way to open it. I knelt down, studying the table legs and sides, looking for anything out of place. I looked underneath the table and saw it; a small wooden knob. I pulled it, but nothing happened, then I pushed it, still nothing.

I examined the button and saw that next to it was a cut in the wood. I held the knob and slid it sideways through the ridge. The table started to shake.

I quickly stood up and saw the water in the glass slosh against the sides. Then the glass started to rise. The square below the flower detached itself from the table, lifting the rose with it.

Below the piece of wood was a crystal the size of a tennis ball, shaped like an opening rose bud. It was clear with specks of black throughout, but along the tips of the carved petals it looked like it was stained red.

Lexi touched the object and chuckled. "It's made of Herkimer diamond. This crystal has a lot of magical attributes on its own without even being enchanted. The power in this is magnificent. This has got to be it!"

"Below the living is the dead," Tristan said. "It wasn't just telling us it was in a cemetery, it was telling us that below the living flower was one that was not living." Lexi reached for it tentatively, then wrapped her tiny fingers around the crystal. She lifted it out of its prison to get a closer look, and the entire tomb started shaking.

16. CRYPTKEEPERS

I'm pretty sure I let out a yelp as the ground shook beneath my feet. Genevieve and Lachlan rushed in then, and Lexi pocketed the stone.

"Come on!" Genevieve called over the commotion and motioned to the door, but before we could take one step toward it, it slammed shut. Lachlan turned and tried to pull the door open, but it appeared to be sealed shut. We looked around at the shaking room, trying to plan our escape when we saw them.

The best way I can describe these things is that they looked like people-shaped shadows. Entirely black, except for their eyes that shone white and small jagged teeth that showed through an unseen sneer. They were by far the scariest things I had ever seen. And there were five of them.

"Shadow men." Genevieve swallowed hard and then resolve settled in her eyes.

They charged at us.

Each shadow man went for a witch. Tristan instinctively ran toward two, knowing that I wasn't in any condition to fight these creatures. He threw a punch at one and shot sparks from his hand at the other. His fist passed through the first form, not fazing the creature, but the other form staggered back from the spell. Only magic harmed these creatures, and Tristan seemed to have figured that out as well. The others caught on quickly. Spells were raining down around me. I pressed myself against the door, watching and trying to stay out of the way in the already overcrowded space.

Genevieve crossed her arms over her chest and then swept them open. The shadow man she fought flew back into the wall. The shadow retaliated; without moving, Genevieve's legs were pulled out from under her, and she fell on her tailbone. She quickly rebounded and cast an icicle spell; pelting her opponent with the frozen shards.

Lexi cast a spell I'd never seen before that shone light blue as it escaped her fingers, vaporizing the shadow.

Before Lexi could let out a sigh of relief, he reappeared in front of her.

Lachlan and Tristan fought back to back, each fighting off their own black mass of evil. The shadows' eyes glowed so bright, the room almost looked completely illuminated. Their feline snarls rang through the room as they attacked, showing their small pointed teeth.

Tristan created a small tornado and it wrapped around the two shadows. With swift movements of his hands he made the two shadows push into each other. As their forms were forced into one by the pressurized air, they exploded in a puff of black smoke. A moment later, they reappeared, ready to keep fighting.

"What the hell is this?" Tristan snarled. "They keep coming back!"

"They must be destroyed three times for it to be permanent," Genevieve called from across the room, still fighting her shadow man. She might have mentioned that before. I wished so desperately that I had my powers so I could help. I knew I would be able to obliterate these nightmarish creatures.

One of the shadow men Tristan had been fighting charged him, forcing him to redirect his full attention to it.

The other found its way to me. I had no room to move back farther, since I was already pressed up against the door.

The shadow man smiled, showing a row of its shark like teeth, and my legs shook from under me. It reached for me quickly, and I tried to evade it, but I was too slow. It pressed its hand onto my throat, lifting me up about a foot, cutting off my air supply. It felt cold and clammy on my skin, raising the hair on my arms and sending shivers down my spine.

I tried to move away, to get some air, but I couldn't. Death had me in its grasp, and there was no escaping it this time. My lungs felt like they would explode from the pressure; my vision darkened around the edges, my eyes unfocusing. I was losing consciousness, and I welcomed it; anything so I wouldn't have to feel this pain. Then I felt warmth spread through my chest, then heat. The creature began loosening its grip, smoke rising from its inky black arms as a burning smell filled the air.

"Selena!" I heard a muffled voice cry, then I saw Tristan fling his arm toward me and the shadow man flew back, pulling me with him before losing its grip and slamming into the opposite wall. I fell to the floor and gasped for air, coughing and trying to open my airways. Sweet relief filled my lungs with each breath I took.

Lexi ran in front of me and created a shield. "Everyone get behind me!" She yelled. The others obeyed. She kept the sphere shield up around us, but stood outside its protective barrier, one hand behind her, holding the shield in place, the other extended in front of her. Blue light shot forth from her fingers into the shadows, making them disintegrate at the touch. Some returned, others didn't. Genevieve shot icicles at the shadows from behind the protection of Lexi's shield, while Lachlan and Tristan spat out fireballs, relentlessly showering the creatures with lethal spells until they were all gone.

The room stilled. The door, released from its spell, opened a crack. The witches stood panting around me, and I was still on the floor.

"Are you alright?" Tristan asked, coming to kneel by my side. I nodded my head, not sure if my voice would cooperate with me just yet. My heart was racing wildly, and my hands shook from either adrenaline or fear, or maybe both. Tristan lifted my chin and observed my neck. I touched my chest where the heat had emanated from and found the necklace Tristan had given me, warm to the touch.

"Guess that works after all," Tristan said.

"Thank you," I rasped.

Tristan shook his head.

I feel useless. I silently sent to him instead. He looked into my eyes.

"There will come a time in the very near future when you will have your powers back. And you will do great things with them again. You'll put us all to shame," he whispered to me.

"I'm sorry you have to keep saving me," I started, and Tristan's eyes blazed with anger. I continued on quickly before he could get mad at me for apologizing. "Thank you," I whispered, still testing out my vocal cords. Tristan helped me up, and we left the tomb in silence. I savored the feeling of the gentle breeze as we stepped out into the fresh night air, and I took in a lungful of it in appreciation.

Lexi walked out a moment later. "I undid the effects of the spells so most of the tomb seems undisturbed. I even managed to close the hidden door of the table. No one will know we were ever here."

Tristan closed and sealed the tomb door and took a step back. "*Now* no one will know we were ever here." He smiled. Lexi rolled her eyes.

"So, what exactly are shadow men?" Lexi asked Genevieve, changing the subject.

"They are created to protect certain objects of great importance. Whoever hides the object creates replicas of themselves so that anyone who tries to steal it will be killed."

"Someone actually looks like that?" I asked, and cleared my throat.

Genevieve chuckled. "No, they replicate their inner, darker selves. The shadow men always end up looking like that though. I suppose when it comes to dark sides, everyone's the same."

You'd think Jeremiah would've given us a heads up on that one, I sent silently to Tristan. It was the easiest way to communicate without the secrecy spell getting in the way. Tristan looked over at me, his jaw clenched, his green eyes glinted in the moonlight, and nodded.

We made sure everything was in order before heading back to the car. Lachlan decided to drive, Genevieve sat in the front and I sat in between Tristan and Lexi in the back.

"I can't believe we did it," Lexi said elated. I smiled. "Aren't you excited, Selena?" She asked me.

"Of course, why wouldn't I be?"

"Well, I just can't see your aura, do you have it reeled in?"

"No, I haven't even thought about it to be honest."

"She's drained from the binding," Tristan whispered to Lexi.

As soon as we were all settled in, I felt a wave of exhaustion overcome me. I could no longer keep my eyes open, all sounds and sights faded around me into blackness.

17. FREEDOM

I woke up when we reached the hotel, but I still felt completely drained. Genevieve and Lachlan went home, and we all thanked them for their help. I showered and got into bed, ready to fall back asleep.

"Finally," Lexi said, jumping into the bathroom as soon as I had finished.

"Selena," Tristan said, standing by my bed. "Are you sure you're alright?"

"Yeah, just tired."

Tristan studied my neck. "That *thing*," he practically spat the word, "left a mark." He lifted my chin and ran his thumb along my jaw as he studied my injuries. He raised his eyes to mine.

"I'm fine, really." I said. My heart rate had picked up a notch though.

Tristan nodded and lowered his hand.

"Get some rest, tomorrow is the big day. Assuming Jeremiah will be able to see us."

I rested my head on the pillow, and the anticipation of what tomorrow held built up inside me. It gave me a boost of energy for all of five minutes before my exhaustion took over.

"Selena, wake up," I heard Lexi in my ear and I wanted to obey but my eyes just would not open. I let out a groan instead. "Come on! We have to get to the courts, remember?" She asked enthusiastically, shaking my shoulder. I was excited to get this spell taken off me, but my body wasn't responding to my inner feelings. Lexi placed her hand under my neck and gently lifted me up.

"She's too weak," Tristan said from across the room. "This spell breaking couldn't come a minute too soon."

I forced myself to move, but my limbs felt like they weighed a hundred pounds each. I was only able to get going because Lexi was holding and supporting me. She helped me to the bathroom and I gasped at my reflection.

My eyes were sunken in, black rings surrounded them. My face looked too thin, and my hair was too flat. It looked like I had been slowly decaying over the past week. I felt like the walking dead, and it was probably true. I was dying from this stupid curse. I was moving so slowly, it took me an hour to get ready, and that was with Lexi dressing me.

I was pissed off. Darien would pay for putting me through this. I walked toward the elevator, my feet literally dragging. I just didn't have the strength to lift them.

Tristan was behind me, "Here, let me help you," he said, and gently lifted me. If it wasn't for the constant movement, I would have fallen asleep right there. This was like the flu times a billion. I fell asleep in the car and Lexi woke me up when we reached the courts.

I walked slowly with Lexi. Tristan strode quickly to the front desk and spoke with the clerk; a scrawny teenage boy with dark hair and an attitude. I couldn't hear them, but the clerk looked stubbornly unhelpful. After a moment, the clerk reluctantly picked up the phone and called someone. He hung up, said something to Tristan and continued on with his work before Tristan even left the counter.

"That punk was telling me I needed an appointment to see Jeremiah. I had to do some serious convincing to get him on the phone. He'll see us in five minutes," Tristan informed us. My heart beat quickly with excitement, but I didn't want my hopes up just yet. After a few minutes, the teenage boy called Tristan over. They spoke for a moment and Tristan came back.

"Okay, we can see him." Tristan led the way, and Lexi and I slowly followed. Tristan reached the door before us and knocked, only entering when he was invited to do so. Inside the room, Lexi sat me down on one of the chairs.

Jeremiah looked me over, his lips pursed in contemplation. "Looks like you made it in time," he said circling me. "I assume you managed to get the object?" He asked.

Lexi nodded and handed the crystal to him. "It would have been nice if we were told about the shadow men," she said after Jeremiah took the crystal.

"Would it now? And what would have been the challenge then? Besides, I think I've told you enough already, don't you?" He asked, admiring the stone. Lexi and Tristan remained silent. "This crystal holds much magic. It is necessary for me to channel its energy for the spell," he explained. "Tristan, would you be so kind as to lock the door please?"

Tristan obeyed. Jeremiah eyed my necklace speculatively.

"What happens now?" Lexi asked.

"Now, I will ask Selena to take off her ring and necklace. Its magic will interfere with my spell. Then," he continued once I had unclasped my necklace and slipped off my ring, handing it to Tristan. "We will begin."

Jeremiah set up candles around my chair and stood in the circle with me. He lit each candle in turn and I recognized that he was calling the elements, though he was speaking in Latin.

Once all the candles were lit, he placed the candle that represented spirit in my right hand, and the crystal in my left. He then began chanting. I had no idea what he was saying, and soon it didn't even matter. The air swirled around Jeremiah and me, but it did not blow any of the candles out. I felt a pressure in my chest that moved down to my stomach. I yelled out in pain, and I saw Tristan take a step toward me before Lexi held him back.

The pressure in my stomach became a scorching hot burning, and I clenched my teeth to prevent myself from screaming out again. I didn't want to scare Tristan. Jeremiah's chanting became louder and more intense, the flames on the candles shot up a foot high, and I instinctively moved the candle away from me. The wind blew incredibly, whipping my hair around my face. The crystal changed from cold to hot and then back several times in my hand.

The air swirling around me moved so fast I couldn't breathe. I sat there, gasping for air. Then I felt it; a release like a brick wall was broken down inside me. I let out a cry from the pain and pressure. An immensely bright light shone around me and seemed to invade my skin. Abruptly, the wind stopped blowing and the candles huffed out, leaving a stream of smoke rising from the wick.

I gasped for air, my hands shook around the candle and crystal. Jeremiah took them from me, and retrieved the candles from the floor. Tristan came to my side and studied my face to make sure I was alright. There was so much worry and concern in his eyes. I nodded to reassure him I was fine. All the pain had stopped.

"Now, you should start feeling better immediately," Jeremiah said. "But you won't feel one hundred percent for at least another hour or so."

"Thank you," I sighed and hugged him. I caught him off guard and he stiffened in response. "Sorry," I mumbled, quickly letting go. He merely nodded.

"Now if there is nothing else, I have other business to attend to." Jeremiah said it so matter-of-factly, he made it sound like this kind of spell unbinding was an everyday occurrence.

Tristan and Lexi took turns thanking Jeremiah and shaking hands, and then we left. I felt alert and awake. I walked out easily, and without needing any help or support.

"How do you feel?" Lexi chirped enthusiastically.

"Much better," I answered just as happily. I saw relief spread across Tristan's face.

"I don't know how I could ever repay you guys for all of your help, or Genevieve and Lachlan." I was so excited! I saw a smile cross Tristan and Lexi's features.

"Someone's aura's back." Lexi grinned. I made a face and reeled it in.

"Guys, I already feel great. Can you imagine what I will feel like in an hour?"

"Well, you never really knew how it felt to have access to all your strength," Tristan told me. "You were still kind of bound when you got rebound, so this will feel amazing. But you have to be careful. Your power is very strong, and you must learn to control it." He pulled out the keys as we reached the car, and I jumped in the back seat. "Here," he said, handing me my necklace and ring back. I went to put them on, but I had this sudden feeling that I just didn't need them anymore.

We stopped for breakfast—or well I guess lunch—and we were able to relax this time. It felt so nice to be able to take in the scenery without the pressure of solving a riddle hanging over our heads.

When we reached the hotel, I bounded down the hallway and stopped at our door smiling. Tristan and Lexi laughed at my new found energy. I couldn't explain the way I felt. Just that I was so happy, and fearless, like I could do or say anything. This was going to be fun! Lexi unlocked the door, and I ran into the room.

"I feel better, but what if it didn't work?" I asked, suddenly hesitant.

"Well, we won't know unless you try," Tristan said. "Just remember that your powers were just unbound, so it could take some time."

"I want to try now." I beamed. I felt like I just had a near death experience and was ready to enjoy life to make up for it. Then again, I guess I kind of did.

"How about you try-" Tristan stopped mid-sentence as I spun my wrist in a circular motion and a small whirlwind materialized between my hands. I wiggled the fingers of my right hand above it, and little drops of water appeared. I stared at the wind and made clouds appear. I then made the clouds collide, and there was lightning. I had my own personal thunderstorm right in the palm of my hand.

"Cool!" I squealed, elated that I had my powers back. I felt complete now. I looked up to see Tristan and Lexi gaping at me, their chests rising with each shallow breath they took.

"Selena. That's amazing," Tristan said in awe, but there was fear in his beautiful green eyes. Lexi stood next to him and licked her lips. The corner of my mouth lifted in a half smile. I was feeling amazing. I clapped my hands together and my thunderstorm vanished. When I looked back at Tristan and Lexi, I noticed something I had never seen before; their auras.

"Wow," I whispered, squinting at the area above their heads. Tristan's was a golden shimmer with a green sparkle running through it, and Lexi's was gold with white sparkles. I felt a sense of peace mixed with an undertone of caution.

"What?" Lexi asked, self-consciously.

"I can see your auras… finally!"

"I have mine reeled in," Tristan said.

"Me too," Lexi added. They had that look again… like I was doing something I wasn't supposed to.

"Do the colors mean anything?" I asked.

"Sort of," Lexi started, "Everyone's auras are different, but we can usually feel the emotion or meaning behind the different hues. They shine brighter when witches use their powers or get emotional... as you know."

I looked for a few more moments, relishing in finally being able to see what they saw, then decided to try using more magic. I missed the feeling of teleporting and wanted to try that next. I closed my eyes and willed myself to the bathroom. I felt the familiar pulling and pushing and opened my eyes. I was in the bathroom, looking at my reflection in the mirror.

My skin looked healthy, with a natural rosiness coloring my cheeks. My eyes were no longer sunken in, the black circles gone. Instead my blue eyes sparkled with something I had never seen in them before. My hair was shiny and healthy, no longer matted flat to my head. I had never looked better in my life, and around me I could see my aura. It was much brighter than Lexi's and Tristan's, but had the similar gold. Only mine also had many other colors as well, each shooting up sporadically. I tried reeling it in, and it diminished significantly. Though even reeled in it was much brighter than my protectors'. Sweet.

I washed my face and walked out of the bathroom toward Tristan.

"So am I at my full power now? It's been almost an hour."

"I don't know, we'll just have to wait and see," Tristan answered quietly. I took a deep breath and exhaled.

"Alright, let's go." I headed for the door.

"Go where?" Lexi asked panicked.

"Out. Let's explore my magic." I am not sure what had come over me, but I was ready to face the world. I didn't have a worry or fear in my body for the first time in my life.

"Tell you what," Lexi started. "I will get us some coffee, and we can work on your magic here, where it's safe. Just until you can understand the limit of your powers," she added when she saw my facial expression.

"If there is a limit," Tristan whispered. I shrugged my shoulders, and Lexi left to get us some caffeine. Not that I needed any, I was already acting like a kid in a candy store.

Tristan sat on the edge of the bed.

"What are you thinking?" I asked, and suddenly I heard a jumble of thoughts. It took me a moment to realize they were Tristan's.

That you are both beautiful and terrifying, he thought, out loud he said, "I'm just amazed at what you're able to do already."

I smiled. "You know Tristan, you're not being fully honest with me. Or yourself. Why do you hold back so much?" I went to him, and he stood, moving toward the window.

"Hold back from what?" He asked, playing dumb, but his thoughts told me something different; *Because I can't allow myself to love you.* My heartbeat raced at that. I was so glad he didn't know I could tell what he was really thinking.

I took a few steps toward him, and he leaned back against the wall beside the window. He stood casually, but I could see in his eyes he was trying to be cautious.

"Come on, Tristan," I whispered, pushing my body against his. He stiffened reflexively. "I know you want me. The sooner you admit it, the sooner we can have a little fun." I ran my tongue along the edge of my top teeth and then licked my lips. I was surprised at my bold behavior. It wasn't like me to be so brave. I liked it.

"Selena, what are you doing?" He asked, surprised.

"Living, Tristan. You have to learn to just let go." I ran my hand along the ridges of his muscular chest and let out a soft moan. "You have no idea how delicious you are, do you?" I asked seductively. Tristan clenched his jaw and grabbed my wrists, holding them firmly away from his chest.

"Selena, stop this. Why are you acting this way?" The fear in his eyes ebbed into concern.

"Do you really have to ask? God, you're oblivious. How do you ignore the sexual tension between us so easily?" I stared into his eyes, boring into his mind.

I can't, he thought. "Selena, you are a very beautiful woman, but there is nothing between us," he said. I clenched my jaw, my breathing became heavy, and Tristan still held my arms. The light on the night stand flickered on and off, my hands shook, and all the doors slammed shut.

"Stop lying to me!" I yelled.

"Selena please, just relax, we can talk this through."

"I'm done talking," I said through clenched teeth. "I know what you're thinking, Tristan, and I know that it's not what you're telling me." I jerked my hands out of Tristan's grasp and tapped my head. "I'm so much stronger than either of us ever imagined."

Lexi walked in then carrying three Styrofoam cups in a cardboard tray.

"What's going on?" She asked. Tristan looked at her and sent silently,

I think she's lost it. Something's very wrong.

I laughed. "Oh Tristan, Tristan, you should block your thoughts," I chided.

"I did," he said staring at me. Lexi's jaw dropped.

Selena, I heard someone call in my head. I was suddenly drawn to the voice. I walked out of the bedroom with purpose.

"Where are you going?" Lexi asked, keeping pace with me.

"To him," I answered in a haze.

"Who?" Tristan asked.

"I have to go," I answered, and walked out the front door. Tristan and Lexi were on my heels.

"Selena, get back in the room," Tristan said. "It's not safe for you to be out here yet."

"I'm done listening to you, Tristan. Unless you have something useful to tell me, shut up." I took the stairs, not wanting to wait for an elevator or ride in it with Tristan and Lexi, but they followed.

I got to the ground floor and opened the door to the lobby.

"Just tell me where you're going." Lexi grabbed my arm to stop me, but I pulled away.

"Wherever he is... leave me alone." I quickened my pace and walked out the front door. Tristan and Lexi tried to follow me when a loud beeping noise sounded. I turned to see security guards coming after Tristan and Lexi. I read the security guards thoughts. Fools forgot to return the keys. I laughed wickedly and teleported to the tempting voice in my head.

I teleported away from Tristan and Lexi and materialized in a forest clearing. Rich green grass grew beneath my feet. Tall, full trees encircled the area, and the sun shone down, warming my skin. I knew I was still in the Hidden City because of the perfect temperature and fresh, clean air. I wondered if I would even be able to teleport out of the city anyway. I then wondered how to leave, but I pushed the concern aside.

Selena, where are you? I heard Tristan in my head. I snarled and ignored him.

I looked around, trying to find the person who had called me before, when a figure came out from behind a tree. As he came closer I recognized his face.

"Darien," I said.

"Hello, beautiful."

A smile crept across my face.

DON'T MISS THE EPIC
FINALE!

FOLLOW SELENA, TRISTAN
AND LEXI AS THE STORY
CONCLUDES IN

UNBREAKABLE

Carol Rayyan is an avid reader of Fantasy and Paranormal Romance who decided to write her own trilogy, and create her own magical world. She grew up in Brampton, Ontario Canada but now lives with her husband Isa, and dog Chewbacca in Scottsdale, Arizona, where she is currently working on her next novel.

Questions or comments? Find her author page on Facebook.com

www.ingramcontent.com/pod-product-compliance
Lightning Source LLC
Chambersburg PA
CBHW020234180626
46810CB00006B/2195